ZIP!

Barney opened the bag, turned it upside down, and bundles of fresh, crisp hundred-dollar bills cascaded out.

Tom picked up a bundle as if he'd never seen money before. "Just like that?" he marveled. "No problems?"

After congratulations, Tom Loder said, "I wonder if we could have hit him for twenty-four thousand like we were going to?"

The idea struck a responsive chord in all of them. "There's no reason why we shouldn't try," Barney said. "Why don't we simply ask for the balance of his account to be transferred? It might be ten thousand; it might only be a couple of hundred, but at least it'll be something."

It was something, all right . . . *One hundred sixty-seven million dollars!* Barney and the boys had one-upped themselves from white-collar crime into international intrigue—and war!

About The Author

Tony Kenrick has previously published three novels. An Australian, he lives and writes on the island of Majorca.

THE SEVEN DAY SOLDIERS

A Novel by
Tony Kenrick

WARNER BOOKS

A Warner Communications Company

WARNER BOOKS EDITION

Copyright © 1976 by Tony Kenrick
All rights reserved

Library of Congress Catalog Card Number: 75-32971

ISBN 0-446-79979-3

This Warner Books Edition is published by
arrangement with Henry Regnery Company

Cover design by Rolf Erickson

Warner Books, Inc., 75 Rockefeller Plaza, New York, N.Y. 10019

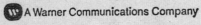 A Warner Communications Company

Printed in the United States of America

Not associated with Warner Press, Inc. of Anderson, Indiana

First Printing: August, 1977

10 9 8 7 6 5 4 3 2 1

For you, Fran. With love and thanks
for all your kindnesses.

My thanks to Major Bruce Jackman, Robin Gabriel, Vernon Howe, the U.S. Army Attaché Office in London —and Major Bruce Jackman again.

When Evil proves impervious to orthodox correction
The remedy doth ofttimes come from a curious
direction.

—16th Century Proverb.

THE
SEVEN DAY
SOLDIERS

Chapter One

It's a well-known fact that nature, the "creative and controlling force in the universe," as Webster's has it, abhors a vacuum. It's also a fact, although less well known, that nature abhors an imbalance. Or too much of one thing and not enough of another. And the way it moves to adjust those imbalances, and the medium it sometimes chooses as its agent, can be very surprising indeed. In this instance—and this is what this story is about—the imbalance was a situation in which there existed a paucity of good and an overabundance of evil, a situation that occurs all too often and so is not in itself very surprising.

But the medium it chose to balance things out was Barney Rivers of Westchester, New York. Which is absolutely staggering. Barney was a punctual commuter, a good family man, was not underinsured, and never would have dreamed of buying a brand of antifreeze that wasn't nationally advertised. Nevertheless, he was the one nature singled out, although he never did realize that he'd been "chosen"—there was no biblical blinding flash, no sudden discovery of engraved tablets. Nature's a lot cooler than that. A lot quieter. Downright sneaky sometimes. Like the way it started the ball rolling at lunch that day in mid-July.

Barney was sitting in the men's bar of a midtown hotel, with huge oil paintings, fake gas lamps, and dark oak paneling around the walls, talking about this and that with a man named Freedman. Bill Freedman wasn't a close friend, but they liked each other's company and usually met for lunch once a month. Naturally they took turns picking up the tab and naturally who ever was owed lunch would make a polite show of offering to pay, an offer that was always firmly rejected.

Except this particular lunch.

When the check arrived, Freedman reached for it but slow enough to allow Barney to grab it off the waiter's tray.

"Oh no," Barney said, smiling. "This is on me."

"Come on," Freedman said, reaching over and plucking it out of Barney's hand. "You paid last time."

Barney shrugged and looked benevolent. "Who keeps score?" He took the check back.

Now this is where that "creative and controlling force" took over. Freedman, in the time-honored tradition, was supposed to say some-

14

thing like "No way" or "Fat chance," at the same time recovering the check for the second and last time. At which point Barney would have graciously acknowledged defeat and the score would have been even. But Freedman, to Barney's surprise and considerable chagrin, didn't do that. Instead he sat back, raised his hands a little hopelessly and said, "Well, if you insist. It's damned nice of you."

Barney managed to keep the smile on his face while he reached for his wallet and mumbled something about it being his pleasure, but it was far from his pleasure. He knew he only had about twelve dollars on him, which meant he'd have to use his credit card and his credit card had lost a lot of its original stiffness from overuse. It was the credit card of a hotel chain and luckily this was the top hotel of the chain. He plunked it down, signed the check and let the waiter take it away. They went on talking, Barney keeping it relaxed and light although he could have cheerfully dumped his coffee over Freedman. The nerve of the guy! He knew damned well it was his turn to pay.

Their conversation was interrupted by the waiter's return. "Sir?"

Barney looked up.

"Would you mind checking with the credit manager, sir?"

"The who?"

"The credit manager. He'd like a word with you."

"I'm having my lunch," Barney said. "What

do I want to see him for?" Although he had a pretty good idea. He tried to remember the last time he'd made a payment on the card. "I'll call him when I get back to the office."

But the waiter wasn't about to go away; he was holding a luncheon check and was responsible for it.

"I'm afraid you'll have to see him, sir, before I can accept this card."

Freedman made a great show of reaching into his pocket. "Here, Barney, let me take care of this."

"Oh, no." The bastard, he was safe enough offering now. Barney scraped his chair back. "I'll see him. He's obviously got me confused with somebody else." He followed the waiter through the tables out of the bar and across the lobby to a door near the reception desk. The waiter knocked, opened it, stood aside for Barney, and left. Barney walked into a small office that was furnished mainly with filing cabinets. The man behind the desk seemed to be in his early thirties, which made him Barney's junior by about ten years.

"Mr. Rivers?" he asked. He didn't get up.

"That's right. I'd appreciate it if you made this fast. I'm being rude to my guest."

The sign on the desk said "J. LANIER" and its owner started with the standard opener. "This luncheon check for twenty-seven twenty. You can't put it on this card."

"Why the hell not?" Barney decided that the strong approach was the best approach. Besides, it was either that or grovel, and Lanier, with his severe face and severe clothes, looked like a man who'd enjoy seeing that.

Lanier picked up a computer printout covered with figures.

"Because your account is in arrears to the tune of three-hundred seventy-eight dollars, Mr. Rivers. Every dollar of that should have been paid three months ago."

Barney wasn't surprised, although it was a little higher than he'd expected.

"That's hardly a fortune. Besides, you're making plenty of interest on it. I don't understand your concern."

"My concern, Mr. Rivers, is that I'm going to have to wait another three months for the money. And I'm not prepared to do that."

"Now wait. Just because I got a little behind——"

"Not a little, a lot. The hotel issues credit cards to people we feel are responsible, but when——"

It was Barney's turn to interrupt. His voice was a little higher this time. And louder. "Let's get this straight now. Are you calling me irresponsible?"

Lanier waved the printout sheet. "Well, what would you call somebody who just lets a debt hang there as if it didn't exist?"

"What do you mean? I've been paying it off regularly."

"Regularly?" Lanier gave the printout paper a vicious flick of his fingers. "Look at this, fifty dollars in March, nothing at all in May, and a lousy twenty-five in June. We can't go on carrying you any longer, Rivers."

That did it. The guy was making him out to be some kind of bum limping along on the hotel's charity.

"Carrying me? Hell, I've been carrying you. Lunch twice a week, drinks after work; I must drop a couple of grand a year at this hotel. What are you trying to do, scare customers away?"

"Only the ones that don't pay."

"Give me that!" Barney snatched up the credit card, bent it, and threw it toward a wastebasket in the corner. "There are plenty of other hotels in this town that'll welcome my business."

Unimpressed by the display, Lanier placed the printout sheet flat on his desk. "Unfortunately, Mr. Rivers, you can't throw this away. I'm afraid I'll need your check for at least two hundred dollars."

"Hell," Barney was steaming. He fumbled in his jacket for his checkbook.

"I'll give you a check for the whole friggin' lot. The entire three hundred and seventy-eight." He grabbed a pen and started to scribble furiously.

"Would you make it out for four hundred and five and twenty cents, please?"

"What?"

"That includes today's lunch."

"Jesus!" Barney scribbled harder, ripped out

18

the check and flung it down on the desk. "There! You satisfied now?"

Lanier picked up the check and examined it. "We're always satisfied when our customers pay their bills, Mr. Rivers."

"Your policy's crazy, Lanier. You just lost a customer for all time. You just said good-bye to two grand a year."

Lanier shook his head. "No, Mr. Rivers. We just said hello to four hundred and five dollars."

Barney was furious at the defeat; the man had insulted him, made him cough up and had beaten him in an argument. There was nothing Barney could do but what he did: reiterate what he thought of the hotel's policy and storm out of the office. He continued across the lobby, stopped at the entrance of the bar, and forced a normal expression onto his face. He went in and threaded his way back to his table.

"Sorry, Bill. They got some card numbers mixed up."

Freedman, not believing a word, got up and said, "Those computers. It happened to me once."

As they were crossing to the door the maître d', who'd been busy elsewhere, caught sight of them and hurried over. "Oh, Mr. Rivers. . . ." His face wore an apologetic grin; the word was obviously out on Barney. "I think the credit manager would like to see you, sir."

It was too much. *"I've seen the credit manager, you dumb farmer, and he's just as stupid*

19

as you are." Barney pushed by him, aware of all the grins around him. And when he had to struggle with the goddamn door, and then found he was pulling it instead of pushing it, and some of the grins turned to outright laughter . . . well, all in all it was a lousy lunch.

Later, back at his desk and cooled down somewhat, his course of action became crystal clear. That little idea he'd had in the back of his mind for ages—just an amusing thought and never in a million years to be considered seriously: He was going to do it.

He had to now.

He had no other choice.

Chapter Two

For once the 5:47 from Grand Central, which was due in at Philipse Manor at 6:27, made it at 6:27. Barney was one of the few who lived close enough to walk home. He moved along the platform, the sun belting into the back of his neck, hot after the air-conditioned cool of the train. Below him the river looked like concrete, not a breath of wind stirring it, not even a boat on it. He slipped off his jacket, climbed the small hill, and turned into Palmer Avenue, the smell of hot pavement and fresh-cut grass in the air. He walked slowly, a tallish man taking long strides, moving with an athlete's relaxation although he'd never been much good at sports. His hair was dark and worn on the long side of short. And while nobody would have described him as handsome—the nose was a little out of line and the mouth a touch too wide, no really outstanding features except maybe the dark brown eyes—nevertheless he had a good face, pleasant and open; "ordinary but kind of groovy" was how one friend of his daughter's had described him. The opinion was shared by most of the wives in the neighborhood. Their husbands found him to be the kind of guy they could relax around, a congenial, mildly witty person who didn't try to tell them how to run their business or insist on giving them stock tips. So Barney was popular and got on well with his neighbors, and one neighbor in particular was very much on his mind at that moment.

He let himself into the front door of a handsome wood-and-stucco house set back from the street, four bedrooms, screened-in porch, good-sized garden in back. He walked through and unlocked the back door. His neighbor on the left, Tom Loder, had beat him home and was sitting where he hoped he'd be, under the tall beech that separated their gardens.

"Hey, Tom," Barney called.

The man looked up and waved a glass. "Come on over. It's post time."

"I'll bring a refill."

Barney shunted between refrigerator and bar and made martinis. A lot depended on Tom Loder. Everything, if what he had in mind was going to work. He finished the mix, picked up the pitcher and a glass, went out into the garden and stepped over the looped wire fence that divided the two properties. Tom Loder held out an empty glass. "You got here just in time. I was dying."

"Yeah," Barney grinned, "I heard about it on the radio and rushed home."

It was a different greeting than either of them was used to. Normally it was a variation of "Hi, hon. How'd it go today?" from their respective wives. But both of their families were at a lake cottage upstate. To cut costs, the two families had decided to take one big cabin for the summer; the plan was for Barney and Loder to batch for themselves through the week then drive up on weekends, and so far it was working out all right. The two men got on well together, partly because they were alike in a number of ways and agreed on a lot of the same things: Both voted a straight Democratic ticket, perferred tennis over golf and thought that Faye Dunaway was what women had been working up to all these years. About the same age as Barney, Tom Loder was a little shorter and bigger boned, and whereas Barney's shirt tucked flat into his belt Loder's rumpled slightly over a spare tire. He had thick dark hair that peaked off his forehead, a nose that hooked downward in the middle, a pronounced jaw; the kind of face that's usually associated with a pipe.

Barney filled his neighbor's glass, then filled his own and swallowed half of it before sitting down. He said, "I've always despised people who say 'Boy, I needed that,' but, boy, I needed that."

"Tough day?"

"Terrible. Absolutely rock bottom." He finished his drink and poured another. "But, it was also a day of decision."

Tom Loder looked at him over his martini. "Yours or your boss's?"

"Oh, no. Not that kind of decision. Something else." Barney put his glass down on the wooden outdoor table, leaned forward, and hooked his hands together. "Tom, what happened to me today was rotten, but I'm glad it happened because it forced me into planning something that, well, if it works, it'll solve a lot of things for me."

Loder waited for Barney to go on, but Barney was thinking about something.

"You can't leave me there. What happened today?"

In quick detail Barney sketched the scene in the credit manager's office. His neighbor wasn't surprised.

"It's pretty cold comfort, Barney, but it's happening a lot lately. They're calling in debts because everybody and his cat seems to be having some kind of cash-flow problem these days."

"Including me. I've got a real lulu right now. I wrote that bastard a check for the full amount. Only thing is," Barney paused, "the check's going to bounce."

Loder looked up at the sky. "Good night."

"I know it. I'll probably get a registered letter from the hotel's lawyers. But the point is, Tom, this is not a temporary embarrassment. I am tapped out."

"You mean it?"

"I spent all afternoon on it. Checked through my figures twice, what I owe, what I earn, what I can raise. It's clear and simple; I'm in the red and getting in deeper every day. And it's a one-way street. Lookit," Barney shifted in his chair. "I'm forty-two. I won't get a raise this year, and it's pointless going after another job because, for one thing, it's tight out there and, for another, I couldn't move for more than I'm making now. I own a handful of stocks that I could sell if I wanted to take a fat loss and I already owe on my life insurance; so that's out. So the only money I've got to look forward to is my salary and it just isn't enough. I'm facing an increasing expenditure on a static income." Barney reached for his drink. "It's a bad time and I know it. Inflation, wage freezes, unemployment . . . a few years ago we lived like most people, always a little over our heads, always spending more than we had. Okay, that's the American way, consume, consume, and stick it on the tab. But it costs too much to run a tab these days even if they'll let you. I guess I figured there'd be a day of reckoning sooner or later, and today was the day."

Barney slumped back, depressed. It was the first time he'd ever really faced up to his situation, even to himself. He seemed to have spelled it out pretty clearly for Tom Loder, too.

"Barney, you're not telling me anything new. I'm in exactly the same boat. I look around me for ways to cut down, but I've already cut down. I quit the club, we barbecue hamburger instead of steaks, I wear my old suits and screw how wide the lapels should be. And we're up at the lake now instead of Montego Bay. And even if I do get a little ahead, something always comes up. I lie in bed at night thinking about it; if I could only get five grand in one spot, five grand that didn't have to be hacked into for Ruthie's teeth or Peggy's new fall coat or a new clutch plate. If I could just get that much ahead, I'd be okay."

The way Barney slapped the table almost spilled the drinks. "Exactly. Five grand free and clear and you'd have a little room to breathe. And I've got a way of getting it."

"I thought you said——"

Barney finished the sentence for him. "No way of raising the money? I don't. Not legally."

It was quiet in the garden, the clack of a lawn mower coming from a few doors away, the occasional sound of a car from the street out front. Barney's last two words seemed to hang in the air in front of them, spinning like a mobile.

Tom Loder said, "Oh-oh."

Barney leaned forward, speaking quickly, confidentially. "Tom, what would you say if I told you I had a foolproof way of getting hold of some money? A simple, no-problem way of ending up ten or twenty grand richer and nobody the wiser?"

"I'd say good luck and I don't want to hear any more."

26

"Yes, you do. You just told me you could use five thousand free and clear."

"Sure. But what I couldn't use is a nice, long jail sentence." Loder picked up the pitcher and noisily swirled the spoon around in it, obviously disturbed by the turn the conversation had taken.

"A jail sentence," Barney said. "That's what stops you, isn't it? But what if you couldn't be caught? What if there wasn't an earthly chance of going to jail, wouldn't that make a difference?"

"Barney, listen to what you're saying. I don't know the first thing about stealing money, but I'll bet you that anybody who ever tried started out by thinking they couldn't be caught."

"We can't, Tom. Believe me, it's impossible."

The way Barney said it and the way he looked saying it forced Loder to ask a question in spite of himself. "What kind of a robbery are you talking about?"

"A bank robbery."

Loder suddenly looked very tired. "Barney, come on now. I thought you had some new kind of wrinkle, something really bright. And all the time you're talking about sticking up a bank."

"No, sir. Not like you're thinking, with the guns and the masks and everybody down on the floor. None of that. In fact, the bank doesn't get robbed at all. Just one person does. One account holder. And even he won't know about it for a week or ten days. What's more, the bank's five thousand miles away."

Loder got quickly to his feet. "I don't want to hear anything more about it. I'm not interested. I'm in data processing, and maybe it doesn't pay as well as bank robbery and maybe it's not as exciting, but at least I can't get arrested for it."

"Okay," Barney said, "you've made your point. I won't say any more."

Loder, his feathers ruffled, slowly sat down again.

"Heard from Peggy?" Barney asked. "I called Elaine this morning. Everything's fine except that outboard quit on them again. I told her she's probably using too much choke, but you know how——"

"Goddamn it." Loder thumped the arm of his chair. "How in hell can you rob a bank five thousand miles away?"

"By mail," Barney said, the sharpness back in his voice. "Listen, this thing occurred to me a long time ago when I was in France. The firm transferred me there for a couple of years; I've told you about that often enough."

"Sure you have. So?"

"So just at that time the French authorities were starting to crack down on foreign residents and their tax situation. So I did what a lot of people did, opened a bank account in Switzerland."

"What, you mean one of those numbered accounts?"

"That's right."

"I thought they were illegal for U.S. citizens."

Barney denied it. "No, sir. Only if you don't

report the fact to Uncle Sam. Then they're illegal."

"So what happened?"

"Well, what I did was simply keep my money outside of France and write the bank in Geneva when I needed money and they'd transfer it to my bank in Paris. That way the French authorities had no way of checking up on how much cash I had around. I didn't have much but what I had I wanted to keep." Loder was leaning forward, absorbed. Barney dropped his voice to keep him that way.

"I used to write for money about every two months, not much, just enough to keep a moderate balance in my Paris bank. Anyway, when I wrote for the money I'd write to the man who looked after the foreign accounts at my Swiss bank, except one day I forgot to include my account number, but the transfer came through just the same."

Loder was right there with him. "So you found out you didn't have to use your account number to get money."

"You got it. Of course, if it's a numbered account only, then naturally you'd have to have the number, but if the account's in your name the right signature's all they look for."

"Okay, I'll take your word for it. Now, how do you apply it?"

"Four steps." Barney counted them off on his fingers. "One, we locate a guy who we're pretty sure has a substantial Swiss bank account."

"Well, you can stop right there," Loder said.

"How are you going to find out a thing like that?"

"He's got a Swiss bank account he's not reporting, right? He's keeping it quiet, not even any correspondence. What he does instead is fly over and visit his money from time to time. Brings some of it back with him maybe. So we look for a guy who travels to Switzerland a lot."

"Okay, go on."

"Two." Barney peeled off another finger. "We get hold of a copy of his signature. Three, I open an account under the name of John Smith or whatever at a local bank, Chase Manhattan say. And four, we write to the major banks in Zurich and Geneva requesting a transfer of ten thousand dollars to the account of John Smith, forging the guy's signature. Now if we're lucky the man we've chosen is going to have an account at one of those Swiss banks we've sent the letter to. A week later the transfer is dispatched to John Smith's account at Chase Manhattan and I, as John Smith with a check card to prove it, simply walk into the bank, write a check, and close my account, which is ten thousand dollars more than it was when I opened it. Bingo, the perfect bank job."

Loder pursed his lips, thinking about it, intrigued but not sold. "What about in Switzerland? What happens after the withdrawal?"

"The Swiss bank sends a notice of the transaction to our man for his records. Our man doesn't understand it; so he either writes or calls the bank to find out what the hell's going on. But by that time John Smith has closed his account and vanished. That's the beauty of this whole thing; if it works we can't be caught and if it doesn't work we can't be caught. So we have nothing to lose and ten thousand dollars to gain." Barney finished the explanation with his arms spread wide and a confident smile on his face, but it still got him a skeptical reaction.

"I don't know, Barney. It's a nice idea on paper but finding someone with a Swiss account . . . how are you going to be sure? A lot of people go to ski and on business and——" His voice trailed off. "I get it." Loder started to nod his head tiredly. "That's why you're telling me all this, isn't it? Because I have access to an entire computer full of facts and figures on a couple of million New Yorkers."

"And also because you're my buddy and can use the money."

"If you can get the money. *If* it's possible to locate the right guy, *if* he happens to have an account at one of the banks you write to, *if* I decide to help anyway."

Barney stood and picked up the pitcher and glass. "Tom, at least think about it. Sleep on it. I wouldn't want you to do anything you felt was . . ." he discarded the word *wrong* . . . "unprofitable. I'll check with you tomorrow." He started toward his house but was stopped by his neighbor's uncertain call.

"It's a lot of ifs, Barney."

Barney raised the pitcher in a mock toast. "It's a lot of money."

31

Chapter Three

Barney wasn't at all discouraged by his neighbor's unenthusiastic reaction; he'd expected it. Tom Loder could never be described as impetuous. He was the kind who liked to sidle into things, to pick a proposition up and examine it carefully against the light before committing himself. Which was all right with Barney. The more Loder looked, the more he'd see how airtight the thing was. The risk wasn't just minimal, it was zero, with a good chance at thousands of tax-free dollars just for trying. You had to be attracted by something like that. And Barney was pretty sure Loder would see it that way, so he wasn't surprised next morning when Loder called him at the office.

"Barney? My lunch date just canceled out on me and I was wondering if you're free?"

"I'm free as long as the lunch is. I ate my wallet for breakfast."

"It's on me," Loder answered. "I'll meet you at Sixth and Forty-second at twelve forty-five."

Barney said he'd see him there and hung up, jubilant. He knew there'd been no lunch date, that was Tom Loder's way of admitting he was interested without actually saying so. And this was confirmed when he met his neighbor later. Loder arrived carrying two brown paper bags, one of which he handed to Barney.

"Tongue and American on whole wheat, okay?"

Barney took the bag and sighed. "There was a time when going to lunch with you meant two martinis and a steak at the Fonda."

"The good old days," Loder said and steered him toward Bryant Park behind them.

In spite of his complaint Barney was delighted with Loder's choice of the park. It meant they could talk without being overheard, which meant that Tom had something to say he didn't want overheard. They chose a spot on the grass bank on the far side, sat down and started on the sandwiches. They'd finished before Loder casually broached the subject.

"Oh, by the way. I had some time on my hands this morning; so just for kicks I ran a few cards through the computer. You know, to see if we could find that guy we were talking about."

"Nothing, huh?"

"You kidding? Bing, bang. Just like that."

"How did you manage it?"

"I just programmed the index for a man in the one-hundred-grand income bracket who

34

doesn't ski and whose firm has no Swiss connections."

Barney raised his eyebrows. "You've got stuff like that on file?"

Loder opened a small carton of chocolate milk and drank from it. "It's not exactly classified information. We make money supplying run-downs on people to mail-order houses, personnel agencies, and so on. You knew that."

"Sure, but I didn't know you could narrow it down so tightly."

"It's not much of a trick. You're only limited by the amount of information you have on a person. The computer pulls out whatever facts you're after."

"But there must be thousands of people who make a big salary and don't ski."

"Oh, I didn't stop there," Loder replied. "We have a copy of the major airlines' executive travelers list. They use it to keep tabs on their first-class passengers. I pulled out everybody who flies fairly regularly to Zurich or Geneva, then cross-referenced them with my original list."

"And that was it?"

"No, I broke them down some more. A bunch of them were in finance-related jobs that could possibly have taken them to Switzerland. I discarded them, also a number in the watch business, as well as some whose hobbies are listed as mountain climbing, alpine touring, and that kind of thing."

"Were you left with anybody at all?"

35

Loder put his hand into his jacket and withdrew a white envelope. "Four to choose from."

Barney took it and opened it quickly as Loder went on. "All four men on that list flew to Switzerland at least five or six times in the last two years and none of them stayed longer than a few days."

Barney ran his eyes over the names, then quietly read them aloud. "Theodore Newman, Donald Kane, Bernard Madison, Arthur Melnik." He looked up. "Bernard Madison. That name ring a bell with you?"

Loder thought for a moment, then said no.

"Is there any chance of getting a breakdown on these guys?"

For an answer Loder handed Barney a sheet of folded paper.

"You've done a fantastic job, Tom. Look at this thing." The sheet was covered with information.

"All I did was run the computer."

"They're going to take over the world," Barney was busy reading the sheet.

"They already have," Loder replied.

"This guy Madison," Barney said. "He's got an impressive record. Corporate lawyer, declared income ninety-five thousand, past president of the Union Club. Conservative Party bigwig. . . ." He looked surprised. "Ex-ambassador, yet. I just wish I could——" He stopped as if a secret message had appeared on the paper. "Bernard James Madison. B. J. Madison. I knew I knew him."

"What?"

"You know him, Tom, the guy who runs those ads in the *Times*, raving on about creeping socialism and how every blind Puerto Rican should get out and hustle."

Loder snapped his fingers. "Got him. That's this guy?"

"I'm sure of it. B. J. Madison." They looked at each other. "Jesus, Tom, he's a natural. He rails against the income tax, can't stand government interference in any form. If he doesn't have a Swiss account, nobody does."

"What about the others on the list?"

"We can only choose one of them and I'm putting my two bucks on Madison."

Loder accepted the decision. "All right. What's the next step?"

"Get a piece of his correspondence. The kind of paper he uses, the typewriter face, the way he words a letter. And his signature, of course. His office isn't far from me; I'll get it this afternoon."

Loder was a little lost. He wasn't used to winging it like Barney; sudden decisions confused him. "You mean walk into his office and take it, just like that?"

"Yes, but with a little more finesse. I don't see why it should be difficult," Barney said.

But that was before he'd tried.

Madison's law office, at the business end of Park Avenue near Forty-sixth Street, had rich mahogany walls, overstuffed, deep-buttoned armchairs, and an oriental rug that covered most of the inlaid parquet floor. It looked like the first-class smoking room of the old *Queen Mary*, and Barney got the impression that it was just as steeped in tradition. The only thing in the room that was less than fifty years old was the receptionist who, while young, was suitably drab and reserved.

Barney said good afternoon to her. "I'd like to see Mr. Madison's secretary, please. My name's Prior. Patrick Prior."

"Do you have an appointment, Mr. Prior?"

"No. That's why I'm here. To make an appointment."

"I see. One moment, please." The girl lifted a phone, pressed a button, and spoke into it. "June, there's a Mr. Prior here. He doesn't have an appointment."

"Tell her I'd like to see her," Barney said, but the girl was listening to the phone.

She took the receiver away from her ear. "I'm sorry, Mr. Prior, but his secretary says you'll have to make an appointment."

Barney gave her a thin smile; she was obviously one of the slow ones. "That's why I want to see her. To make an appointment."

"He says he wants to make an appointment with you," she said into the phone.

"Not with her, with Madison. But I want to see her to make it."

"He says he wants to make it with you."

They were interrupted by the arrival of an older woman whose sharp manner and tailored suit said "executive secretary."

"May I help you, sir?"

"Please. My name's Prior. I'm trying to see Mr. Madison's secretary."

"Do you have an appointment?"

"No, that's what I'm here for. To make an appointment."

The woman took the phone from the receptionist. "June, there's a Mr. Prior here. He's arrived without an appointment."

"I didn't arrive without it; I never had one."

The woman was scribbling on a pad. She hung up. "August ninth," she said. "Is four P.M. convenient?"

"That's three weeks away. I can't wait three weeks. Look, if I could just see her myself."

The woman stood staunchly in his way, implacable guardian of the firm's highways and byways. "I'm sorry, sir. Mr. Madison's a very busy man. That's the earliest date we can give you."

Barney made a small gesture of defeat and turned to go. The woman snapped around on her heel and vanished through a side door. At that moment the receptionist's phone buzzed, she answered it, hung up, picked up a pad and pencil, went through the same door, and left the office deserted. Barney didn't hesitate. He turned and walked quickly toward the main door and almost into the young man coming through it.

"Oh, excuse me," the man said. "May I help you, sir?"

"I'm fine, thanks. Mr. Madison's expecting me. I'll just go on in."

39

"It'd be better if I announced you, sir." He picked up the phone. "You have an appointment, do you?"

"Yes I do," Barney said. He turned wearily back toward the corridor. "But I'm a little early."

Chapter Four

"**I** was so bad, Tom. You wouldn't believe how bad I was. I couldn't even get past the outer office."

Loder, sitting opposite him under the beech tree, tried to gloss it over.

"Don't hate yourself, Barney. I know what some of those old established law firms can be like. They operate on connections, introductions. A guy walking in cold like you did is going to get the runaround."

Barney nodded, looked miserable. "The thing of it is, I thought locating the man was going to be the hard part. Instead it turns out that getting one of his letters is the hang-up."

Loder mulled it over out loud. "Even if you wrote Madison, tried to get a letter from him that way, I guess his secretary would reply for him. I can see the problem."

"Tom, we need somebody to get us a letter.

We need a good thief. You know any crooks?"

"Only my TV repairman."

"I mean it, Tom. We need a pro."

"How do we get one?"

"I don't know. Do we know anybody who comes in contact with them?"

They looked at each other, both a touch embarrassed. Apart from a little creativity with their tax return each year, people in their position, solid middle-class commuters, had nothing to do with anybody who operated outside the law. They seemed to be stymied.

The whole thing might have ended right there if it hadn't been for something that happened just then, something so ordinary that neither of them gave it a second thought: Their neighbor, George Dourian, whose house adjoined the two back gardens, wheeled his car into his drive and went into his front door. It didn't really register with Barney except in his subconscious. He moodily bit his lower lip, brooding. Finally he stood up.

"Well, so much for the big heist."

Loder tried not to show his disappointment. "It was a sweet idea, Barney. You were killed by a technicality, that's all."

"I guess so." Barney started to move away then stopped abruptly as the message zinged into his frontal lobes. "Dourian," he said softly.

"Who?"

"George Dourian. Do we know anybody who comes into contact with thieves? George Dourian."

42

Loder didn't get it right away and Barney spelled it out for him. "At his job. He runs a department store, doesn't he? And what are department stores famous for? Shoplifters."

"Hey." Loder got up, too. "That's not bad. Hell, he must brush up against them all the time. And a smart shoplifter's just the kind of guy you want, in and out of Madison's office just like that. Barney, I think that's it. That is," Loder added, "if George will go for it."

"Sure he'll go for it. Two ex-wives to support and that house to pay off? He'll eat it up."

"Maybe so. But he'll still have to come up with the right person. Somebody reliable."

Barney smiled at the thought. "A reliable shoplifter. I like it. Come on, let's go and see him now."

"Both of us? I haven't said I'm in this thing yet."

There were times when Barney wanted to grab Tom Loder and shake him by his lapels. "Just come along as an observer then."

Loder didn't see anything wrong with that, and together they walked to the end of the garden, stepped through a gap in the hedge, and went around to Dourian's front door. It was opened a minute later by a man with a very dark scowl on his face.

"Hi, George," Barney said. "Have we come at a bad time?"

George Dourian waved the piece of paper he held in his hand. "Anytime's a bad time when you get something like this in the mail. Four hundred bucks for a new boiler! I ask you, where in God's name am I supposed to find four-hundred American dollars?"

His two callers glanced at each other.

"George," Barney said casually, "I think I may just be able to help you there."

When Barney finished outlining the scheme, pacing restlessly up and down Dourian's living room, the reaction he got surprised him. George Dourian, thirty-eight years old, just sat there sunk into the sofa, his eyes flicking back and forth between Barney and Loder, who was sitting on the edge of his chair. It was uncharacteristic of Dourian to remain silent; he always had something to say, usually loudly. Impulsive, quick and mercurial in his moods, he was a man of extremes, down one minute, up the next, either leadenly pessimistic or unshakably optimistic. These traits had involved him in two disastrous marriages, both entered into on the spur of the moment and both heartily regretted not long after. Part of the problem was Dourian's inherent attraction to women. He was a big man, rangy with a solid, hard body that had been coordinated well enough to get him onto the football team at Columbia. Hearty would have been one way of describing his general appearance; he had thick black hair, curly and lots of it, a broad forehead, high cheekbones, an eyebrow line that formed a straight ridge across his face, a mouth that showed a lot of teeth when he smiled. He seemed

44

to radiate an aura of self-possession that a lot of women were drawn to; a kind of emanation that tweaked a responsive chord in them. However, at this particular point in time, all that was emanating from Dourian was a pensive quiet, which Barney mistook for an expression of doubt.

"So there it is, George. You don't like, huh?"

"You really want me to tell you what I think?" Dourian asked.

"Give it to us straight."

"I think," Dourian said quietly, seriously, "that it's the best damned thing I've ever heard of."

"But . . ." Loder said, anticipating a qualification.

"But nothing." Dourian jumped to his feet, his voice rising with his body.

"It's fantastic! Beautiful! And it's going to work like a charm."

"Then you're in?" Barney asked.

"You kidding? Up to my eyeballs. Christ, I've been looking for something like this for a year, what with inflation and the slump and those two bloodsuckers I'm supporting, and my stocks so low I can't see them anymore. Man, I've been racking my brains for a way to get ahead, and here you are right next door with the answer. Barney, you're a gold-plated genius."

"Hold it. Hold it a second," Barney said. Dourian's penchant for instantly embracing something was as unsettling, in its way, as Tom Loder's fence sitting. "Thanks for the nice words and we're delighted you like the idea, but we're not bringing you in on this just because you're a pal."

Dourian's grin shortened a little. "Well, sure. Naturally. Tom came up with the guy's name and you'd like me to help with something. What?"

"A shoplifter."

"A reliable one," Loder added.

Barney didn't give him a chance to comment on that but jumped in and described the debacle in Madison's office.

"So we need somebody to steal us one of his letters. A pro. And seeing as how you run a store and have to come into contact with shoplifters, we figured you could get us one who'd do the job."

"You mean catch one in the act and force him to help us?"

"Something like that, yes."

Dourian sat down to consider it. "Shoplifters are normally security's job. I mean we don't have store detectives as such; we contract a private firm. When they catch somebody, they handle it themselves. I don't have much contact with that side of things, but I guess I could bring myself in on it." He was thinking out loud. "I'm the manager, after all. I could have a crackdown on theft and make sure I got to see anybody they caught. The only problem then would be getting somebody we'd feel happy about. Somebody reliable, as you said."

"Right," Loder nodded. "Some little old lady

trying to grab a pair of socks isn't going to be any use to us. We need somebody cool who can keep his mouth shut."

"It'll mean cutting him in," Barney said, "which will reduce the take all around. But if we don't let him share he could turn around and blackmail us."

There was general agreement on that point.

"You think you can swing it, George?" Barney asked.

"I'll give it a damn good try."

"Can you start tomorrow?"

"Why not?"

"Then that's it," Barney said.

Dourian walked them to the door, the grin back on his face.

"It's a great idea, Barney. A winner."

Barney shrugged off the praise. "It'll either work or it won't. The main thing is there's going to be no nail biting in this. No risk, no sweat. And no repercussions if it goes wrong."

No risk. No sweat. No repercussions. Later on they reminded Barney that he'd said all that.

Especially the part about the repercussions.

Chapter Five

The store Dourian managed was in a recently opened shopping plaza in Hartsdale, a very high-class shopping plaza designed to be a miniature Fifth Avenue. The shoe store was modeled on Bergdorf's, the bookstore stocked only hardcovers, the kitchen shop sold nothing that wasn't from France, and the lowest-priced wine in the liquor store was five dollars. In the center of the plaza a tiled fountain splashed and the walkway was all red glazed brick. It was very nice, very Westchester. Dicken's, Dourian's store, was a small and very select fashion store that had positioned itself, pricewise, somewhere between Magnin's and Saks. It was housed in a white, double-storied building that sported Florentine arches at the front entrance and had a less decorative rear entrance from the parking lot.

When Dourian got there the next morning the first thing he did was meet with the security people. He explained how the management was on an anti-shoplifting drive, that they were to really keep their eyes peeled this week, and that he wanted to personally interview anybody they caught. He issued the same instructions to his department heads, then retired to his office to work and await results that, however, were very slow in coming and very disappointing when they did come.

He knew that shoplifters usually came in waves, but that week the tide seemed to be out and the only thing that came into his net was the little old lady Tom Loder had spoken about, this one caught with a size twelve swimsuit stuffed down her umbrella. There was also the usual weekly case of a Scarsdale matron who haughtily claimed she'd been on her way to the cash register with that pants suit; no charges pressed in either case. So the following Monday, when Barney and Loder got back from a week-end with their families at the lake cabin, Dourian was forced to give them a gloomy report. But they decided to give it another week, and two days later their patience paid off.

Dourian had gone around the store again late in the afternoon giving a pep talk to the security men and also talking it up with the sales staff. The saleswomen all wore a uniform—dark skirt and candy-striped blouse with their name tag pinned on, except the department heads who wore smart, simple dresses, and it was to one of these Dourian was speaking.

"Anything. Anything at all suspicious, Miss

Berg. A shopper hanging around, anybody with a shopping bag they bring in, and particularly keep an eye on the dressing rooms."

The woman darted her eyes around the store. "I understand, Mr. Dourian."

He moved off around the floor, urging eternal vigilance on any of the saleswomen who weren't busy with customers. He stopped one of them, who was walking by with a pile of dresses in her arms.

"Oh, miss. . . ." He read her name tag. "Miss Skelton, is it? You're new, huh?"

"Yes, sir. I started yesterday."

"Your floor supervisor brief you on shop-lifters?"

"Yes, she did," the young woman said.

"Right. Keep an eye out; we're cracking down."

The woman nodded and moved away, and Dourian walked back to talk to the department head again.

"I've had a word with most of the women, Miss Berg. They're on their toes. Oh, incidentally, let me know when you hire somebody new. I like to know the staff."

Miss Berg, thin and fiftyish, peered at him through peaked horn-rims. "I haven't hired any new people, Mr. Dourian."

"Sure you have. Miss Whatshername. Skelton."

"There's no Miss Skelton in my department, sir."

Dourian looked exasperated. He didn't need this. "I was just talking to her. Nice-looking girl.

51

Had a big pile of . . ." His voice went lame ". . . dresses in her arms. Oh, my God."

Miss Berg stared as he took off, crossed the floor, and raced down the escalator. He ran through the street floor and out into the parking lot. There wasn't a sign of the young woman, but he heard a car door slam and on his left an orange Volkswagen rocked slightly as somebody got into it. He ran toward it as the engine started, caught a fast glimpse of a pink-and-white blouse, thrust his hand through the window and whipped out the key. The engine died.

"Miss Skelton," he said, getting his breath back, "do you always drive to the stockroom?"

She slumped in her seat. "Shit," she said.

Dourian opened the door. "Come on. Bring the dresses."

She gave him a tired look but got out and scooped up the dresses laid out on the back seat. Trying to look as inconspicuous as possible, Dourian guided her to the entrance and up the escalator. Miss Berg was nowhere to be seen; so he took the dresses from her, hung them on a rack, and led her to his office. He pointed to a chair. She flopped into it and sat looking at her hands.

"Where did you get the store blouse?"

"Alexander's. On sale."

"And the name tag?"

"I had it made up. There's no law against that, is there?"

Dourian sat down opposite her. "No, but there's a law against stealing a dozen dresses."

"Eight dresses."

"There's a law against that, too." She didn't say anything and Dourian looked her over. That was pretty smart, dressing like one of the saleswomen. Who was going to ask a saleswoman where she was going with a pile of merchandise? She'd have gotten away with it if he hadn't spoken to the department head when he did. Nice-looking kid, too. Face a little on the slim side maybe, and the mouth could have been fuller, but thin lips were kind of sexy. Nice hair, too, corn-colored and shiny. Definitely a good-looking chick. And a smart one.

"What are you, about twenty-five, twenty-six?" he asked.

"What?"

"Skelton isn't your real name, is it?"

"Look. You got me cold. So call the cops because I don't have to tell you anything."

"What's your real name?"

She sighed. "What's the difference?"

"I like to know the people who rob my store."

"Atwill. Amanda Atwill. You happy?"

"Well, Miss Atwill," Dourian picked up a pen from his desk and moved it between his fingers as if he were testing a fine cigar, "let us review the facts here. I've caught you cold, as you point out. So I merely have to call security who will call the police who will arrest you for theft. I'm just guessing but I'll bet they'll have seen you before. Anybody who goes at it like you did is no amateur. And if they've seen you before, you've probably been convicted before; so another conviction wouldn't do you much good. Am I right?"

She tried to look bored. "If all that's supposed to mean I'm going up this time, you're right. So why don't you stop gloating."

"I'm merely getting the facts straight. And if those are the facts, I have two alternatives. One, I call security and they press charges, and two, I don't call security and there are no charges."

The woman frowned, suspicious. "You mean just let me go?"

"On condition," Dourian said.

"On what condition?"

"That you do a little favor for me."

She traded in the suspicious look for one of cynical weariness. "I get it. One of those, huh?"

It was a second before Dourian caught on. "Just a minute. You're not reading me right. I'm talking about a different kind of favor."

"I didn't know there was one."

Dourian leaned toward her. "Miss Atwill, what would you say if I told you that I knew how to dip into somebody's bank account without the slightest risk of getting caught?"

She was surprised but recovered quickly. "I'd wonder why you were telling me."

"Sure, but apart from that."

"I'd still wonder why you were telling me."

"Maybe because I need your help. In return for which I'd be willing to cut you in."

Amanda Atwill blinked at him. "This is pretty rich. I get hooked for one rip-off and offered another rip-off? What do I have to do?"

"Steal a piece of paper."

She gave him a sidelong glance. "What kind of a piece of paper?"

"Just an ordinary, everyday business letter." When there was no comment, Dourian said, "I'm offering you a way to make a lot of money with no possible chance of going to jail. The alternative is not make a lot of money and almost certainly go to jail."

"That's not much of a choice, is it?"

"It's not meant to be."

She turned her palms up. "Well, I'm sure as hell not about to put myself behind bars, but I'm going to have to know more about this thing. A lot more."

Dourian thumped his desk; he'd got her. "Agreed. I have two associates in this with me. I'd like them to take you through it; it's their idea." He glanced at his watch. "They'll be home soon, why don't we go meet them? That is," he added for the sake of politeness, "if you're free right now."

"You mean if I want to stay free right now."

"Come on," he said, "let's go."

They left the office together, by a side door, locked her car, and took Dourian's back to Philipse Manor. During the drive, he tried to draw her out, but she answered only in monosyllables and he could see that, while she knew she was getting off lightly, she didn't like the fact that she'd been boxed into a corner. But she opened up a little when he wheeled the car into the driveway.

"Hey," she said. "You live here?"

"Yes, ma'am."

"Nice."

"So are the payments."

Dourian let her in the front door and she preceded him down the hall. She stopped when it opened into the living room.

"Oh, yes." She looked round, taking it all in. "That's a Kaprolan rug, isn't it?"

"I don't know. One of my wives chose it."

She turned to him. "How many do you have?"

"Two. Both ex. You want a drink? I'm going to have one."

She followed him into the kitchen and was stopped by this room, too. She walked around touching things, impressed. Dourian started on the drinks and made another attempt at drawing her out. It worked better than the first time.

"Where are you from?"

"Jackson Heights."

"You live there now?"

"I live on the West Side now."

"You married?"

"Nope."

"Live alone?"

"Nope." The way she said it and the glance she gave him told him that she wasn't sharing with her sister. "I wouldn't like to live by myself."

"Try it some time," Dourian said. "It's heaven." He handed her a drink.

She ran her eyes over the chrome of an infrared stove. "Those two wives of yours, it couldn't have been easy leaving all this."

"I don't get it," Dourian said. "I thought all this was supposed to be a symbol of male repression these days. Aren't you into the women's movement?"

She made a quick dismissive gesture with her free hand. "The movement doesn't really apply to me. Every woman should have a career, they say. I already have one."

"What is it?"

She looked at him, surprised. "I'm a booster. What did you think, a typist?"

"Oh, sure. Sorry, I was forgetting. That's what you call your department-store work, isn't it? Boosting."

She nodded and tasted her drink. They sat down at the counter.

"Tell me," Dourian said. "Do you always work alone?"

"Now I do. I used to work with a couple of guys, but they blew a job and got caught."

"How did that happen?" He wanted to keep her talking, loosen her up, get her over the feeling that she'd been forced into something. He wanted her in on the job because she wanted to be, not just to escape a jail sentence. Although that possibility, he realized, was fast disappearing. Nobody takes a shoplifter home for drinks before having them arrested.

"It was a fiasco," she said. "I was supposed to go into this men's store, walk up to the counter, open my coat, and say 'Look.' When the clerks looked the two guys were supposed to clean out a rack of suits. I was naked under the coat."

"Naked," Dourian repeated.

"So the clerks would look."

"Yeah, I figured that. So what happened?"

"Those two schmucks I was working with." She raised her eyes to the ceiling in painful memory. "They looked, too."

Dourian smiled. It was perfectly understandable. Now that he'd had more time to study her. A nicely curved fullness to her blouse and. . . . His mind was snapped back to business by the phone ringing. It was Barney calling to check on any progress. Dourian told him to come on over. When he arrived at the back door a few minutes later, he had Tom Loder with him. Dourian went outside and told them what had happened.

"A real piece of luck. I caught her myself; so nobody knows anything about her."

"It's a her?" Barney asked.

"Very definitely."

"I might have guessed," Loder said.

Dourian led them inside and made the introductions and they moved into the living room.

"I thought it best if Miss Atwill heard it from you, Barney, seeing it's your baby."

Barney launched straight into it, told her exactly what they planned and how it was supposed to work. "Tom here got us the name of the pigeon, a creep called Madison. He's rich enough so that he won't miss the money and you can feel good about robbing him because he spends a fortune running unkind ads in the newspapers. But to write those letters to the Swiss banks we need an example of his style and signature. Do you think you could get into a law office and lift a few letters?"

The challenge didn't faze her. "I hit Macy's once for three typewriters in two days. I should be able to boost a couple of letters."

"But don't forget," Barney warned, "this place is harder to get into than Macy's."

"Sure. But I'll bet it's a lot easier to get out of."

It was a good answer; Dourian could see that both men were pleased with it. And with Amanda, too. They wouldn't have to take a vote on her; she was already in.

Barney was talking again. "If it all works out, we'll split four ways. So if we tap him for say, twenty-five grand, that's a little over six thousand apiece. That okay with you, Miss Atwill?"

"You kidding? I only got fifty dollars for the typewriters."

Barney gave her the name and address of Madison's office, then declined Dourian's offer of a drink in favor of going back and calling his family at the lake. Loder said he'd get in on the call, too. They wished Amanda luck and left.

"Nice guys, aren't they?" Dourian said, coming back from the front door. "And isn't that a sweet little idea?"

The girl agreed. "It's nice to work with smart people for a change."

"Believe me," Dourian said, "you wouldn't catch those two stopping to look when you opened your coat."

She looked at him sharply.

"What I meant was——"

She waved away the explanation and looked for her purse. "You want to drive me back to my car? I'd better get back and think about how I'm going to get into that office." She saw his hesitation. "Don't worry, I'm not about to run out on six thousand dollars."

"It's not that. I was thinking. Instead of going all the way back to Manhattan, why don't you stay here?"

"In your house?"

"Sure. There are four of us in on this deal and three of us live next door to each other. It'd make a lot more sense if all of us lived next door to each other."

When she didn't kill the suggestion right away, he pressed on. "I don't know what kind of arrangement you've got over there on the West Side. . . ."

"Loose. Very loose."

"Then stay. You just said you want to think about how to get into that law office. It's nice and quiet here and there'd be no interruptions."

She ran a hand over the soft suede of the sofa. "Well, I don't know."

"You can have my wife's bedroom. It has a lock on the door. It also has its own bathroom with a shower massage from Hammacher Schlemmer."

"Really?" Amanda said. "Hammacher Schlemmer?"

Dourian had said the magic words.

So Amanda moved in and they were all set. They had the plan, they had the mark, and they had a professional thief they could depend on. Things looked good. And before they got worse, they got better.

Chapter Six

At 8:44 the next morning, Amanda was riding her first-ever commuter train and forty minutes later was walking through the door of her first-ever corporate law office. She was carrying a large box wrapped in brown paper. On it, in large black Flomaster, was written "Mr. B. Madison, 10th Floor, 242 Park Avenue." Underneath that, in letters that couldn't be missed, was "By Hand." The receptionist wanted her to leave it, but Amanda insisted that it be delivered personally. Ten seconds later she was through the door that had proved impenetrable for Barney and making a beeline for Madison's secretary, a snip of a woman with a thin line for a mouth and hair shorter than a man's.

"Good morning," Amanda said. She took a fast look at the desk top, chose her spot, and thumped the package down. The side that showed was the reverse of the one the receptionist had seen. "Boy, that's heavy."

"What's this?" the woman snapped.

"By hand delivery for B. Madison, two forty two Park."

The woman made an irritated noise with her teeth. She stabbed a finger at the package. "That stupid girl, this is for a Mister B. Park, two forty two Madison."

Amanda checked. "By golly, you're right. I don't think I'm out of bed yet."

She started to move off. "Sorry to trouble you."

The secretary sniffed and swung back to her typing. She didn't miss the letters Amanda had picked up with the package for a good half hour. But by that time they were on a train heading for Philipse Manor.

When Dourian got home, later than usual, he found a number of things in his house that hadn't been there when he'd left. Barney and Loder, an electric typewriter, a ream of paper, some envelopes, half-a-dozen ball-point pens, and a bunch of business correspondence.

Amanda explained. "His secretary uses an IBM; so when I got back here this morning I called a local rental shop and had them deliver one. The letters are typed on Hammermill bond and he signs his name with a ball point; so I picked up those at a stationery store. Also the same kind of envelopes he uses."

Dourian looked at the stuff, then looked at

Amanda. "You did all this in one morning?"

"How about that?" Barney said. "It took me almost that long just to make an appointment."

Amanda turned the praise aside. "It was a breeze. No store dicks to worry about." She moved toward the kitchen. "Excuse me. I'll go check on the lamb."

"What lamb?" Dourian asked.

"I had the store send around some food. I hope you don't mind. I figured you guys could use a break from all those frozen chicken pies."

As she left the room, Loder said to Dourian, "You just *found* her in your store?"

Dourian had a large grin on his face. "I know. It's more like I won a national contest."

Barney sat down at the coffee table and started leafing through the letters. "These are great, a real good selection. One to a newspaper, one questioning a bill. . . ." He read them over. "His style doesn't change for any of them. Terse and cold. I'll bet he even signs himself 'Yours Sincerely' when he writes his mother."

Loder took a look. "That signature doesn't look too hard; it's almost copperplate. And the ball point's got to make it easier."

Barney put a blank sheet of paper in front of him and scribbled on it with each of the pens Amanda had bought.

"That one," Dourian said. "The thin point."

"It figures," Barney said. "The guy wouldn't even lash out in ink." He looked up. "Anybody had any forging lessons?"

Loder suggested they all try. When they

compared handwriting, it was no contest; Loder's try at Madison's signature was by far the best.

Barney started working on the text of the letter. He thought and scribbled, thought some more and scribbled some more, then read it out.

"Listen to this. 'Dear Mr. whatever his name is, I would be much obliged if you would transfer, at your earliest convenience, X number of Swiss francs from my current account to the account of blah blah at so-and-so bank. Yours sincerely, etcetera.' How does that sound?"

"How can we tell?" Dourian asked. "All we heard was a lot of blah blahs and so-and-sos."

Loder came in with a question. "What about those names? How do you know who to write to in Switzerland?"

Barney reached into his jacket and unfolded a piece of paper. "I made four calls to Zurich yesterday, one call to each of the four big banks. I just asked them for the name of the officer who looks after the foreign accounts in Zurich and their Geneva branch." He showed them the list. "There it is. Credit Suisse, Swiss National Bank, Union Bank of Switzerland, and Banco Allemagne Suissa. And the names of the officers at each."

"What if Madison has his account at some other bank there?"

"Then we're out of luck. But if he has an account at all, you can bet it'll be with one of the four majors. He's not the kind to take a flyer."

They all went along with that. Loder asked

him how he planned to handle the bank at this end.

"I'm going to open an account tomorrow at the Stuyvesant State Bank. The Bronxville branch."

"Why that one?"

"No particular reason, just that I've never been inside any of its branches and Bronxville isn't a part of the world I spend much time in. If this thing goes through, I don't want to meet the manager on the street the next day."

Loder asked him what name he was going to use.

"MacDonald. Steven R. MacDonald. Nothing fancy, a nice, ordinary name."

"All right," Dourian said, "let's hear the letter with all the names in place. Use the first name on the list. Go ahead."

Barney obliged. "Dear Mr. Klienzle, I would be much obliged if you would transfer, at your earliest convenience, seventy-two-thousand Swiss francs from my current account to the account of Steven R. MacDonald, Stuyvesant State Bank, Bronxville, New York. Yours sincerely, B. J. Madison."

Amanda had come back in while he was reading. "How much is seventy-two-thousand Swiss francs?"

"Last time I looked the rate was around three to a dollar; so we're asking for something like twenty-four grand."

"And if he doesn't have that much in his account, what happens then?"

"The bank will write and tell him and the ball game will be over."

Amanda considered it. "So the less we ask the more chance this has of working."

"She has a point," Dourian said. "We don't want to price ourselves out of the market."

"Okay," Barney said, "what are we willing to settle for?"

Tom Loder spoke. "I'd rather have five grand I could count on than miss out trying for six."

"Then what do you say we ask for twenty grand, which makes it sixty-thousand francs?"

They all agreed.

"Then that's it. I'll open that account tomorrow, and tomorrow night, if Tom's ready with that signature, we'll type the letters, mail them off, and see what happens."

Barney told the office he'd be late the next morning, drove over to the bank at Bronxville and, as Steven MacDonald, opened a checking account. While he was doing that, Amanda, who'd done half a typing course once, typed up the letters and Loder, after spending most of the previous night perfecting Madison's signature, signed them. Barney mailed them the following day. He figured the transfer would take about a week to ten days; so there was nothing for any of them to do except wait. He and Loder went back to the daily routine of their nine-to-five jobs and spent the weekend up at the lake swimming and fishing with their families and acting as if they weren't in the middle of an international bank robbery.

Dourian and Amanda, on the other hand, started up a different kind of daily routine and soon, as a not too surprising by-product of sharing the same house, embarked on a nightly routine, too. One night, in bed together, they stopped what they were doing long enough for Amanda to ask a question. "Hey," she said between small bites of his shoulder, "how does it feel to make love to a rip-off artist?"

"Sinful," Dourian replied. Although, in point of fact, Amanda's shoplifting bothered him. She'd needed clothes and since he hadn't wanted her to go back to the West Side apartment to collect them, he'd offered to outfit her at the store at a trade discount, but instead she went over to Saks and got herself an even better discount. But the time passed quickly for them and they were surprised when Barney dropped in one night and announced that he was going to call the bank the next day. Neither of them gave it much thought, unlike Barney, who couldn't sleep thinking about it.

He was bleary-eyed and had butterflies dancing in his stomach when he called the bank at lunchtime from a phone booth near his office.

"Good morning. My name is MacDonald, Steven MacDonald. I'm expecting a transfer from Switzerland. I wonder if you'd be good enough to check if it's arrived yet."

"MacDonald," the voice said. "Just a moment, sir."

Now that he was finally down to the wire, Barney was filled with doubt. Stealing twenty grand just couldn't be as simple as he figured. It was fine in theory but in practice something was bound to come up. Either the man would say it hadn't come, which might mean that Switzerland was checking with Madison before releasing the money, or he'd say there was a slight discrepancy and could he perhaps drop into the bank sometime soon, which would mean they knew the fix was in. Or——the man's voice cut into his gloomy thoughts.

"Hello, Mr. MacDonald? It arrived yesterday."

"Yesterday," Barney repeated in a dulled voice.

"Yes, sir. Approximately twenty thousand dollars from the Banco de Allemagne Suissa in Zurich."

Barney heard himself thank the man, then hung up. He stepped out of the phone booth and stood on the sidewalk. "Hot damn," he said softly. His delight only lasted a minute and was replaced by a more pragmatic reaction. He checked the time, walked to Forty-second, went into the big Rexall and bought an overnight bag. He hurried down into the Lower Concourse and caught a local to Bronxville. The bank was just around the corner from the Gramatan Hotel and Barney stopped in front of its doors. This was the hard part. Before it had all been anonymous, untraceable—you couldn't go to jail for opening a bank account under another name—but now he'd be physically laying hands on money that wasn't his. Stealing. What if they were waiting for him in there? What if that phone call had just been a come-on. The alternative was to turn around, walk away, and never know for sure.

He took a deep breath and a firmer grip on the bag and pushed through the bank's doors.

Dourian and Loder knew the moment he walked in. Dourian's face broke like a sunrise. "You're kidding!"

Barney zipped open the bag and turned it upside down over the sofa. Bundles and bundles of fresh, crisp hundred-dollar bills cascaded out.

"Jeez-*us*!" Dourian yelled. He grabbed Amanda and swung her around.

Tom Loder picked up a bundle as if he'd never seen money before, then looked at Barney as if he'd never seen him before, either. "Just like that? No problems?"

Barney shrugged. "I saw the manager, wrote out a check, and the teller cashed it."

There followed a good ten minutes of mutual congratulations, during which Dourian opened the bar and everybody got a little glow on.

"Twenty thousand dollars," Dourian said for the fifth time.

Then Tom Loder said something, a casual remark tossed off lightly, that started the whole enterprise sliding into the mire.

"I wonder if we could have hit him for twenty-four thousand like we were going to?"

It wasn't just Loder's fault; the idea struck a responsive chord in all of them.

"I'll tell you what," Barney said. "there's no

reason why we shouldn't try. We know his bank; we could fire off another letter asking for an additional transfer."

"Wait," Amanda said. "When will that Swiss bank notify Madison about this transfer?"

"Two or three weeks. Probably three. It's just a record of the transaction. So a second letter will get to Switzerland in plenty of time."

"What the hell," Dourian said. "Let's go for broke. Let's ask for another ten grand."

Loder waved a hand. "Too much. We may have already drained him dry. Let's settle for the original four thousand, an extra thousand each."

There was a pause. Then Barney spoke into it, a slow smile stretching the corner of his mouth. "I've got a better idea. Instead of specifying an amount, why don't we simply ask for the balance of his account to be transferred? It might be ten thousand or it might only be a couple of hundred, but at least it'll be something."

Everybody thought that was a great idea. So Barney composed another letter, Amanda typed it, Loder signed it, and Dourian sealed it. And the next day Barney mailed it.

It was a preliminary act that could be likened to a man who was shortly to be mauled by a tiger shark, diving into the warm crystal water and starting to swim.

Chapter Seven

When Barney called the bank a week later, he wasn't surprised when they had nothing for him, and when he got the same answer two days running, it was pretty clear that their little game was over. All the same, he gave it one more try the following day.

"Hello, this is Steven MacDonald. I called yesterday."

"Oh, yes, Mr. MacDonald. Landman here, assistant manager. About your transfer isn't it?" Barney noticed something strange about the man's voice, a thin nervousness as if he were being careful of what he said. "It's arrived, Mr. MacDonald. It's here."

With his heart giving a little jump, Barney wondered how long it took to trace a call from a phone box.

The man was speaking again. "Sorry it took

so long. We had to check back with Switzerland. We thought there might be some mistake."

"Oh, God," Barney thought, "they've transferred a dollar forty nine all the way across the Atlantic." In an embarrassed voice he said, "Mr. Landman, I don't have my records in front of me. What was the amount again?"

There was a cough on the other end of the line. "In round figures, Mr. MacDonald, we have credited your account with just over one hundred and sixty-seven million dollars," the assistant manager said.

Chapter Eight

Philipse Manor's reaction to the news was similar to Barney's: bewildered shock followed by a rocketing euphoria that burst very quickly and fell back to earth as the ramifications became apparent. Except for Dourian. His euphoria was still on the rise.

"Forty million dollars," he kept saying. "I'm worth forty million freaking dollars." His impromptu dance in the middle of the carpet was shifting into a higher gear when he noticed that, far from getting up and joining him, everybody else was slumped around looking worried. Slowly his dance wound down, then stopped altogether. He looked from face to face. "What is it?"

It was Amanda who answered. "Something's wrong, George."

"What could be wrong with forty million dollars apiece?" He searched the faces again.

Whatever it was, they were certainly all in agreement.

"We checked Madison out," Barney said. "Tom and I even went over and took a look at where he lives. A big ranch-style number in Mamaroneck. Very nice. Two cars, one's a Lincoln. He looks like what he's supposed to be, a successful lawyer pulling down a hundred thou a year. So what's he doing with a bank account of a hundred and sixty-seven million dollars? In short, who is this guy?"

Dourian sat down, as sober as everybody else now. "It's not his money."

"I'm damned certain it's not his money. The question is, whose money is it?" There was a very heavy silence; then Barney pulled out a piece of paper he'd been carrying around with him. It was the profile Loder had given him. He began to read from it. "Bernard J. Madison. Born Evanston, Illinois, 1910. Graduated from Williams, then Harvard Law School, started Liston, Roache, junior partner four years later, then a long stretch with Seeforth, Burns Associates, active Conservative Party fund raiser, appointed ambassador to Cabrera 1958. Returned to this country 1960 and made full partner, Seeforth, Burns." Barney lowered the paper. "Cabrera. A little island in the Caribbean, isn't it?"

"Near Jamaica, I think," Loder replied. "Why, do you think there's something in that?"

"I don't know. They had a revolution down there, I remember that. But there was something else." He tapped the paper against the coffee table and frowned at it. Then he looked up. "Is the library open tonight?"

"Could be. I think it is."

Barney got up and moved to the telephone, checked the number of the local library, and made the call. They listened while he asked a librarian for some information on Cabrera, then waited for her to find it. It took the best part of five minutes, a silent, nervous five minutes.

"Go ahead," Barney said and started to make notes on a telephone pad. Halfway through he raised his eyes to them. It was the kind of look that normally accompanies a piece of disastrous news. He resumed writing, said thank you, and hung up. He walked to the sofa, sat down, and gave it to them straight.

"In March, 1957, Luis Ripoll, a lawyer who was formerly minister of the interior, became president of Cabrera and ruled as dictator till October, 1960, when a guerrilla band, modeled after Castro's, came down from the hills and overthrew him. Most of the embassies closed and the ambassadors were recalled, including the U.S. ambassador, pending recognition of the new regime. Ripoll escaped to Paraguay and was later accused of absconding with gold reserves then valued at forty-two million dollars."

Barney looked up from his notes and saw that he wouldn't have to repeat any of it.

In a flat voice, Loder said, "Gold's gone up about four times since then. So there's your hundred and sixty-seven million dollars."

Barney tossed the pad onto the table and sank back into the sofa. "Ripoll didn't want to risk putting that money under his own name because even a numbered account is no protection if you're investigated. So he had his good buddy, the U.S. ambassador, open an account for him. Bernard J. Madison is a bagman for the ex-dictator of Cabrera. Which means we have stolen the treasury of an entire country."

Nobody gave Barney an argument; that had to be the way it was. The enormity of what they'd done overpowered them.

Dourian gave a nervous bark of a laugh and ran a hand through his mop of hair. "This thing, it's kind of got out of hand. We started out to steal a little money from a guy who could afford to lose it so we wouldn't feel bad. Fine. But we end up stealing from an impoverished island. I don't want to bleed all over you, but places like Cabrera, they're all dirt poor."

"Then we'll have to give the money back," Amanda said.

Loder winced. "Wait. I feel the same way. I'm not trying to play Robin Hood, but if I robbed poor people I couldn't sleep nights. But if I just walked away from a fortune I wouldn't sleep nights either."

Barney stared at the blank TV screen as if the answer were going to be presented to him live. The screen stayed blank but his brain came on.

"What if we sold it back to him? What if we contacted the guy and offered him his money back for a price. That way we could feel good about it and still end up rich."

Amanda threw her hands in the air. "How could we feel good about giving the money back to the man who'd stolen it?"

"Because he wouldn't end up with it. Look, we tell him that in return for a million dollars' cash we'll transfer the money back to him. If we make a mistake and it's transferred to Cabrera instead, then it's up to Ripoll to go back and claim it if he wants to."

"Very cute," Amanda said. "But the million dollars comes off the money that belongs to Cabrera."

"No, it would only have been earned by that money. Even at the low interest the Swiss banks pay, Ripoll would still have made a fortune on it. You could call it a finder's fee."

Loder came in with a warning. "It's smart, Barney, but it could be risky. An ex-Caribbean strong man is going to know a few tricks. We'll have to figure out how to pick up the cash without him picking us up."

"There are a lot of things we'll have to figure out," Barney said. "But before we do anything, I think we should do a little research. Find out what we can about this guy so we know who we're dealing with."

"You volunteering to fly down to Paraguay?" Dourian asked.

"I don't think I'll have to go any farther south than a Hundred and Tenth Street. Go down to the Barrio, find a few expatriates, and see what they can tell me." He looked around for a positive reaction; nobody looked very hopeful. "I'll go tomorrow. If I hear terrible things, then we'll forget the deal and send the money back to Cabrera." He smiled at them. "Look," he said, "at the most all we've got to lose is a hundred and sixty-seven million dollars."

In the accurate predictions department Barney wasn't exactly leading the league. And his newest prediction didn't do a thing to help his average.

Chapter Nine

Like most Westchester residents the farthest
north Barney ever traveled in Manhattan was
83rd Street when he took the kids to the Metro-
politan on a rainy Sunday now and then. Otherwise his view was limited to a glance out of the
window when his train emerged from the tun-
nel around 125th. Or on those rare occasions
when he drove into Manhattan and found the
East Side Drive closed, he got a closeup of the
Barrio driving down Lexington, windows up and
doors locked tight. His attitude toward Spanish
Harlem was a fairly typical one: It disturbed
him that it was there and that so many of its
residents were so badly off, and it was arguable
whether it had to exist at all. But since it did,
he accepted it. It was there like the East River
was there or the George Washington Bridge—
part of New York. Still, his acceptance of the
Barrio didn't make him feel any better about

going into it, and he was relieved when he only had to enter the southern fringes. It didn't have the boisterous life of the main section on the East Side, with its wildly colored shopping stalls and eating stands sizzling away, the crowded fruit and meat markets and the record stores blasting out a solid wall of sound; this part was quiet, sleepy almost. The sun seemed to have sucked all the energy out of the air and the streets had a limp, plastic look to them. Barney had figured that the best way of checking on Ripoll would be to talk to an ex-resident of Cabrera. He'd checked with a magazine on the restaurants that featured Cabreran cooking and they'd given him three names. The first one, a place called La Pastilleo, had familiar beer signs written in neon script in the window and an unfamiliar legend printed on the window itself: *"Comidas Criollasy Chinas."*

He went in, sat down on a bar stool, and looked around. The place had a grubby prettiness about it that was cheerful at first glance, depressing if you looked hard enough. There were the usual pictures of Spanish sports celebrities signed and framed behind the bar, an unswept wooden floor, a radio tuned to a Latin station, and signs on one wall hand-lettered and trimmed in what looked like aluminum foil. They listed such dishes as Caldo Gallego, Cedo Chop Suey, Polla Asado, and a few others Barney had never heard of. At one end of the bar two men were talking, taking turns slamming a leather dice box down onto the wood. Three of the tables were occupied, three groups, all of them men, eating with very little talk. The bartender folded his newspaper slowly and put it down on top of a cigar box that held bottle tops, can openers, pouring spigots, and a small, faded American flag. Barney ordered a beer and started to talk to the man. The bartender's English was fluent, although heavily accented, but it soon became clear he wasn't going to tell Barney anything he didn't want to.

"You from Cabrera?"

"*Si,* Cabrera."

"Reason I ask," Barney said—he'd decided just to come right out with it—"is because I'm trying to find out a little about Luis Ripoll."

It was only fleeting, but Barney got the impression that the name had stopped everybody for a moment. Then the dice box slammed down again and he wondered if he'd been wrong.

"Ripoll," the barman repeated. He was a heavy man, shiny black hair, thick mustache, thick stumpy fingers. "I don't know this guy."

"Come on, he used to run your country."

The man blinked slowly and shook his head. "I'm a kid when I leave Cabrera. I'm in Miami twelve years. Out on the Trail there. Then I come here. I don't know this Ripoll."

"Uh-huh." Barney half turned on his stool. "Well, maybe one of these gentlemen can tell me something."

"You got Spanish?"

"A little high school stuff."

The bartender shrugged. "These guys only got Spanish."

It was a lie and Barney knew it; either they didn't want to talk about Ripoll or they just wanted the gringo out of there. Barney paid for his beer, put down a tip and left. Nobody looked up.

He got the same kind of treatment at the next place he tried, the bartender claiming he was Cuban and knew nothing about Cabrera.

The third place the magazine had given him looked like a frost, too. It was almost an exact replica of the other two bars, same shabby-bright decor, same sweet, spicy, frying smell that was making Barney feel hungry. The bartender in this one admitted being from Cabrera but said he'd only been eight years old when Ripoll had been overthrown, a fact that Barney couldn't argue with. He was getting up to leave when the man came over to take his money and mumbled something that Barney at first thought was in Spanish. It was only when he was outside on the sidewalk that the words clicked into place. The man had said, "Come back around ten."

He killed the time after the office closed by catching up on some work he'd been neglecting, then left the office at eight and dropped into a movie. It was a waste of money; he was too preoccupied and he finally left and strolled up to

96th Street and got a cab through the park.

At the restaurant the same bartender noted his entrance with a fast "*Ola*" and, with a flick of his eyes, indicated a table in a far corner of the room. The place was a lot more crowded than it had been at lunch. All but two of the dozen tables were occupied by families, little kids running around them with bread in their hands, younger ones stuffed into high chairs, their mothers shoveling food into them. All the husbands and the older children were stolidly eating away as if the others at their table had no connection with them. In the corner, eating by himself, was a man whose fair hair made him a standout. Barney moved through the room and stopped in front of him.

"Hello there," Barney said.

The man looked up, chewed and swallowed, and nodded at the empty chair. He seemed to be expecting him. "Sit down."

Barney accepted the offer.

"You eaten?" the man asked. Barney said he hadn't and the man called a waiter and gave him a fast burst of a language that sounded like Spanish with all the ends chopped off. Barney commented on it; it was as good an opening as any.

"You speak the language pretty well."

"I was ten years in Cabrera. It took me seven years before I could speak it like they do."

The waiter noisily set a place for Barney and thumped down a short glass tumbler, which his host filled with wine. Then the waiter reappeared with a heaped plate and Barney picked up a fork and tried the food.

"It tastes kind of Chinese."

"It is kind of Chinese. Cuba adopted Chinese cooking and blended it into their own. And whatever happens in Cuba sooner or later happens in Cabrera."

The man got busy with his own plate and Barney picked up his wine and took a closer look at him. About his own age he judged, with a static kind of face, bland and pale like his hair except for the eyes, which seemed to look through you when he spoke to you. His body looked narrow and long; bony shoulders under the Spanish-style shirt that was ribbed on both sides and worn outside the pants. There was a solidity about him in spite of his slimness and a confidence that wasn't necessarily accounted for by his command of the language or his obvious comfort in the restaurant. He appeared to be a man who'd decided on a particular approach to life a long time ago and was following it in an unwavering line.

"My name's Gage," he said.

"Rivers," Barney replied before he knew it was out of his mouth.

The man saw Barney's mistake but didn't comment on it. He forked up some food and ate for a moment. "I hear you've been asking about Luis Ripoll." Barney, too quick with his first answer, went back to his plate and said nothing.

"You a cop?" Gage asked.

"No."

"Journalist?"

"No again."

"Then what's your interest?"

"I want to contact him about a personal matter. But before I do that I'd like to find out something about him. All I know is what the official biographies say."

Gage finished a last mouthful then pushed his plate to one side. He brought his wineglass in front of him and leveled his eyes on Barney's.

"They won't tell you much. This country supported Batista a lot longer than it propped up Ripoll. Check the official entries on Batista. Cuban dictator's about all they say, with the dates of his rise and fall. They don't say too much about the corruption and the police terror."

"Is that what they'd say about Ripoll if they could?"

Gage's eyes were level and very steady. "Why do you want to know? Tell me the truth."

"I have something that belongs to him. I think he might be interested in buying it back." The man had told him to tell the truth and, Barney realized, he'd done just that. There was something about the man that seemed to inspire it.

"How much are you asking?"

"Why? Are you interested?"

"I'm interested in anything that can hurt Luis Ripoll."

The way Gage said it, firmly and openly, caused Barney to shoot a fast look at the next table. "I got the impression," Barney said, "that people were scared to talk about him."

"So they should be. Ripoll's a butcher. He'll kill anybody. That's the way he stayed in power. If anybody said anything against him or even if he just thought they had, there were no threats, no warnings, you just died. He still operates the same way."

"Still? In Paraguay?"

"Ripoll left Paraguay six months ago and came to this country."

"They let him in? But how about that gold he was accused of stealing?"

"Never proved, Mr. Rivers. Besides, a man who runs a country for a couple of years makes friends in high places. Useful when you're after a little thing like an immigration visa."

"Where does he live now?"

"About ten blocks away."

"Ripoll's in *New York?*" The information shook Barney. It put a whole new complexion on things, a very frightening and immediate one. Barney had come to ask questions, but he hadn't expected the answers Gage was giving him. Barney drank from his wineglass and got his thoughts together. He asked another question.

"You've told me the man's a killer, yet here you are telling a perfect stranger you're out to get him. Why aren't you afraid of him?"

The answer was delivered flatly. "He won't touch me now; he's already touched me. He had my wife killed. And my two sons. He left me

alive so that every day I could wake up and remember I don't have a family anymore."

The waiter arrived to clear the table and filled
in the silence with the clatter of dishes. He
poured the last of the wine into their glasses and
went away.

Numbed by what Gage had just told him and
not knowing what else to say, Barney asked how
long ago it had happened.

"Four months ago."

Barney shook his head, bewildered. "I don't
understand. What possible threat could you be
to him here? Why did he do it?"

Gage sipped his wine, picked up a paper napkin and dabbed at his mouth. Then he scrunched
up the napkin into a tight ball and held it in his
fist. "Because I told the truth about him a few
years ago. That was his excuse, anyway. But the
real reason was because he loves having the
power of life and death. He spent three years as
virtual emperor of two million people, sole
judge and jury. I think he misses that. There are
no Cabrerans in Paraguay but there are fifty
thousand of them here, more than in Miami
even. So he came back to rule them." He tossed
the napkin onto the table and pushed his chair
back. "Shall we go? It's getting hot in here."

They went out into the summer night and
walked west, Gage silent now, letting Barney
assimilate what he'd told him. Now that they
were outside, with the traffic going by, people
around, and street noises, everything Gage had
just told him sounded unreal, a fantasy. Yet

Barney knew it was true. There were people like Ripoll in the world; what was hard to realize was that he was now very much involved with such a person. He wanted to ask Gage about the killings and about his family but didn't dare to be so unkind. But the man volunteered the information.

"You ever heard of the Pachones?"

"No."

"When Ripoll ran Cabrera, he gathered around him an elite corps of palace guards, mainly ex-police thugs. From them he chose forty of the best and most trusted as his bodyguard. They became known as the Pachones. A pachone is a hunting dog. They were his safeguard against assassination as well as a weapon of vengeance. When the revolution came, some of them were caught and strung up, but twenty-five of them escaped with Ripoll to Paraguay. He brought them all to New York."

"Twenty-five. That's a private army."

"A very vicious private army. They're well named, Mr. Rivers. They're animals, subhuman. Every one of them has tortured and killed dozens of people. Literally. The one who killed my family"—he said it matter-of-factly—"is called Manolo. He's known as Rabidosa because he's mad." They stopped at the curb and Gage looked at Barney, his face expressionless. "You wonder how I can talk about it, don't you? I can talk about it because it'll be my turn one of these days."

A light changed and they moved across the

street. Barney said, "You told me Ripoll was living around here. Where?"

"The Hotel Maria on Broadway. He has the entire fourth floor, the Pachones live with him and go everywhere he goes. He'll be going to the track tomorrow; he goes every Saturday. So if you want a close-up, he usually leaves the Maria around one."

They'd stopped outside a faded red-brick tenement with people sitting on the fire escape like birds nesting in trees, radios going, people drinking beer. Gage said, "This is where I live. Not exactly the Hilton but I like to stay close."

"Look, if I want to talk to you again, where can I reach you?"

"Here, second floor right. Or at the restaurant." He hesitated for a moment, his eyes searching Barney's face. "Rivers, I don't know what your game is, but I'd take it somewhere else. Don't get involved with Ripoll. And don't trust anyone who is."

Barney watched him climb the stoop and disappear through the broken front door. He got a cab to Grand Central, got onto a train, and sat waiting for it to start, trying to think the thing through. It was hopeless; he had his head deep in the lion's mouth; if he wanted to keep it from being snapped off he'd have to very quietly tiptoe away. There was no question now, of course, of trying to make any money out of this; he wasn't going anywhere near a man like Ripoll. They could kiss that money good-bye. It was a slow trip home on the local. When he got into his front door, the phone rang. It was Tom Loder, who'd been waiting for him, and Barney told him to come over. He appeared a minute later, his face very grave.

"Barney, I've got some bad news."

"It couldn't be as bad as I've got."

Barney filled him in on his meeting with Gage, and Loder listened without comment, waiting till Barney was through. When he did say something, it was a real stopper.

"If everything this guy says is true, Barney, it makes my news disastrous." He held up the newspaper he'd brought in with him. "You see the *Post* tonight?" The paper was opened to an inside page, and he pointed to two photographs of a man that were butted up against each other. "It's an item about somebody who pulled a bank job in disguise. Look at the caption under the shots."

Barney read it out loud. "Two faces of Jepson. Mug shot and bank surveillance photo."

"Bank surveillance, Barney. We forgot about the cameras. You told me the manager okayed that check and you cashed it at the teller's window. Barney, you're on tape."

Barney's only reaction was to close his eyes for a long moment. His voice, when he spoke, had no alarm in it, just a tired acceptance. "You're right, Tom. Goddamn it, they know what I look like. I should have thought of those bank cameras. Even so, it's not the end of the world. They'd never trace me from a photograph."

"You're wrong, Barney. Remember Don Briloff, used to live over on Crescent Drive? I ran into him last week. We had a fast chat, the 'you're-looking-well' kind of thing. I asked him was he still at First National and he said no, he'd switched banks." Loder stopped there; he didn't have to add which bank the man had gone to. Barney said it for him.

"He's at Stuyvesant State."

Loder nodded. "We've had it. Once Ripoll finds out that his money went to a Steven Mac-Donald at Stuyvesant State in Bronxville, all he has to do is check with the manager. They'll run the tape for the day you withdrew the twenty thousand and the manager will identify you. They'll pull out the frame, blow it up, and start checking. When they get nowhere with police files, they'll start checking other banks, their own branches first. And when they show that photograph to Briloff, it's all over."

"But Ripoll would have to tip his hand. If he goes into that bank looking for Steven Mac-Donald, he'll have to admit that it's his money. He won't risk doing that."

"I've thought it through, Barney. There are a number of ways he could check without giving the game away. Look, Madison will receive the notification of the twenty-thousand-dollar transfer in maybe ten days. He'll check back with the bank and they'll tell him about the balance being transferred, too. Madison goes to Ripoll and Ripoll gets moving. And one hour after your photograph is put in front of Don Briloff, Ripoll will be knocking on your front door. And if he's anything like this guy you met tonight says he is, God help us all."

Barney reacted with a kind of negative panic. His face blank, his movements slow and heavy, he got out of his chair and walked across to the fireplace. He spent a long time looking at the watercolor that was framed above it before he spoke.

"Okay. The first thing we do is check out Gage's story. We'll go into town tomorrow and take a look at Ripoll for ourselves so we'll know what we're dealing with."

"And then?"

"Try to figure some way out."

"What do we tell George and Amanda?"

"Nothing. Let's not tell them a thing till we know our position. It may be possible to make some kind of deal with Ripoll, I don't know. But I think it's pointless bringing the other two in until we know where we're at."

Loder stood up. "Gage told you Ripoll goes to the track Saturdays?"

"He leaves the Hotel Maria around one. Let's try for the eleven forty. I'll call Elaine in the morning and tell her we won't be up this weekend. I'll think up some excuse."

Loder okayed that, said he'd see Barney in the morning, and started for the door. Barney stopped him.

"Tom, it's probably stupid to say this but, believe me, I'm sorry."

"Don't feel bad, I'm the one who came up with Madison."

"And I chose him." Barney's laugh was more of a grunt. "I thought he was going to be so easy. Instead he turns out to be the worst guy in the world to rob."

"Maybe not so bad. Let's wait and see what Ripoll's like. This guy Gage is probably wildly exaggerating."

"Sure," Barney said. "Probably."

The Maria was a large commercial hotel built in the twenties when the Upper West Side still had a touch of class. It lost money on accommodations now and barely made it up catering to local weddings. Not a month went by that a rumor didn't spring up that the place was going to be torn down to make way for a supermarket or an entertainment center or a discount furniture mart. But the rumors always proved to be just that and the Maria went on being a fifty-year-old white elephant, a little seedy, a little rundown, but still with a residue of glamor left over from the days when people came uptown to the clubs wearing tuxedos and evening dresses. It had two entrances, front and side, and Barney and Loder had positioned themselves opposite the side-street entrance.

"Barney, I don't buy it. If Ripoll's so rich, why does he live in a dump like this?"

Barney squinted into the bright sunshine bouncing off the pale brick of the building. "According to Gage, a lot of people in this section are from Cabrera. Ripoll's still playing dictator and this place is his palace."

"Maybe," Loder said, doubtful. "And maybe he was spinning tall tales for the wide-eyed tourist."

"No, you weren't there. Gage was for real."

"Well, he was wrong about him going to the track at one. It's twenty five after and where is he?"

The question was answered immediately. A large black Cadillac swung around the corner from Broadway, rolled five yards past the hotel entrance, and stopped. It was followed almost immediately by another that pulled up on the other side of the entrance. Car doors slammed and, although they didn't seem to have hurried, ten men stood on the sidewalk flanking the hotel doorway. They appeared casual, lazy almost, but their eyes swept the street, checked the parked cars, checked the windows above the little colmado grocery that Barney and Loder were standing outside. They were struck by the similarity of the men, as if each one had been chosen for his resemblance to the next. They were all of medium height, broad and big-chested, with dark, Hispanic features. Their clothes differed very little: loafers, dark slacks, tan or cream-colored sports jackets over open-necked shirts. Most of them wore big Cuban-style dark glasses. But the single most striking detail was the uniformity in their expressions: flat, hard, cold; a complete absence of anima-tion, as if their facial muscles were paralyzed. On the balcony overlooking the entrance, two more of them appeared. They stood on each side of the balcony, back from the rail, looking down and around, watching. A third Cadillac rounded the corner and swung into the space between the first two, directly in front of the entrance. Like the other two cars there was something thick and heavy about the way it moved, as if it were towing something. There was a moment of stillness on the street, then the doors of the hotel opened and Ripoll came out surrounded by a circle of men. Barney got only a fast glimpse of the man but it had to be him: big, broad shouldered, graying hair, expensive silk suit. The group seemed to melt into the waiting car and, as the doors closed, a fourth car came up alongside it as a shield until the men on the sidewalk were back in their cars. The whole convoy moved off together, slow and ponderous at first, then picking up speed and wheeling into West End Avenue. On the balcony the two men moved inside.

Barney started to speak, coughed on a dry throat, then tried again. "Twenty-four men. Twelve in the first two cars, five in the last one, five in with Ripoll, two on the balcony."

"I've never seen anything like it." There was a note of awe in Loder's voice.

"It was so smooth. Ripoll couldn't have been on that sidewalk for more than a second." He was about to say something more but didn't get the chance. Somebody was calling Barney's name.

"Mr. Rivers. . . ."

A cab pulled up in front of them. The man in

the back opened the door and told them to get in.

"It's Gage," Barney said.

They got in and the cab started off.

"I thought I'd find you here," Gage said. He introduced himself to Loder who said hello but sidestepped an exchange of names.

Barney asked him where they were going.

"I want to show you something." He flicked his eyes toward the driver and they said no more. The cab traveled only a few blocks. Gage paid the cab and they waited till it had moved off, then started back the way they'd come.

"You saw Ripoll and the Pachones?" he asked Barney.

"Yes, we did. I didn't know how much to believe of what you told me; so I came down to check."

"That was smart of you. But I think I can help convince you. We go in here."

At first Barney thought the tenement they entered was the one Gage lived in, but then he realized this wasn't Gage's block, although it couldn't have been far. The streets and the buildings had the same happy-sad look to them, the hung washing making bright splashes of color against grimy brick. The big difference was inside: There was no noise. No radios, no TVs, no kids playing, no people in evidence anywhere. The silence seemed thicker and heavier than the lingering cooking smells that covered an older smell of staleness and age.

They followed Gage up three flights of stairs

and along a dim corridor. He stopped before an apartment door and knocked. The door was opened a crack by a somber-looking old man who recognized Gage and stepped aside. The apartment was tiny and not much lighter than the corridor—religious pictures on the patched wallpaper, plaster saints on a black sideboard, photographs of children in Communion clothes, lamps with ridiculously frilled shades, a huge, velvet-covered sofa in the shape of a blob. In a corner, sitting at a formica-topped table, two men were watching another who sat like a statue, eyes closed tightly.

Barney threw a questioning look at Gage, who said, "How many Pachones were with Ripoll just now? Twenty-four?"

Barney nodded, wondering what was coming.

Gage moved them across the floor and opened a bedroom door. "The other one was up here," he said. "Manolo. I think I told you about him."

The bedroom had a thick, sweet smell and a murky underwater light, and for a second it was hard for Barney and Loder to know what they were seeing. Then the shapes took form and the sudden recognition sucked the breath from their mouths.

There was a cracked washbasin on the wall. Barney stumbled to it and was violently, horribly sick.

Chapter Ten

Barney had finally drifted off to sleep in the early hours of the morning, only to wrench awake again thirty minutes later, the sweat chilling his body. He stayed up until the sky began to change color, then fell asleep with the lights on and stayed that way till nine o'clock. Then he dressed and walked out into the fresh morning. He thought that the new day would soften the clarity of the image stuck in the projector of his memory, but it kept popping back in front of his eyes: the woman sprawled on the bed, the knife slashes running the length of her naked body in parallel diagonals. The two little children like ripped rubber dolls. And the crib in the corner with the pathetic pool of blood underneath it. He cursed Gage for not preparing him for the sight. It had been too ferocious an education, too harsh. They'd told Dourian and Amanda about what they'd seen;

they knew it would horrify them, but they were past the point of holding anything back now. They told them everything so they'd know exactly the position they were in. They'd all agreed to think separately about what they were going to do and meet at eleven that morning. Barney hadn't been able to think about a thing except the scene in that dim little apartment. He knew that wasn't good enough; he'd gotten the others into this, it was up to him to get them out.

He went inside, made coffee and drank two cups black. Then he went around to the garage and got out an old hand mower. He began to push it over the grass of the back garden, cutting it in long, even swaths, doubling back on his track and catching the edge of each freshly mown aisle. He enjoyed the precise symmetry of it, as if the green fountain spraying from the mower blades might wash away the picture that kept trying to form in his head. Little by little, he found himself able to think. By eleven, the grass unfinished, he went inside, drank a lot of water, and came out again toweling his face. He crossed into Loder's garden and sat under the beech and was joined by the other three, all of them in poor shape—especially Loder, whose eyes were red-rimmed and sandy-looking. There were no greetings; Barney just began talking.

"I've thought of something that may or may not work, but it's at least a course of action worth considering. Before I get into it, has anybody else got anything?"

Nobody had.

"Okay. A couple of things occurred to me for a start, probably the same things that occurred to you, and you probably nixed them for the same reasons I did. One, we pack a suitcase and take off to Europe or somewhere, which is no good because we'd only be waiting for the door to crash open one day and one day it would. So hiding's out. Two, we could go to the police and level with them. Problem is we'd go to jail and anyway Ripoll would reach us there, too. Also our families would be left unprotected; so giving ourselves up isn't the answer." Barney mopped the sweat on his forehead, not all of it earned by cutting the grass. "As I see it, the only way we're going to get out of this is to buy our way out. We have to make a deal with Ripoll."

Loder started to speak, but Barney waved him down. "I know what you're going to say Tom; Ripoll's a man who's not used to making deals; and you're right. But however you cut it we've still got his money. We've got something he wants. What I'm proposing is that we offer to give it back to him but on our terms."

Barney paused for questions, but they were waiting for him to continue and he spoke a little faster. "This is how I figure it. For starters we get out of here, lock up the houses and go upstate somewhere and tell nobody where we're going. That'll give us a safe base to operate from. To make it doubly safe," he looked at Loder, "we'll move Elaine and Peggy and the kids to another cabin. That way Ripoll won't be able to get to us through them. And," he said, switching his eyes to Amanda, "I think it would be a good idea if you joined them."

"Absolutely," Dourian said. "I want her out of this."

Amanda didn't like it. "I'm in this as much as any of you. There has to be a way I can help."

"No," Barney said, "not with what I've got in mind. I'll get to that in a minute." He turned back to the two men. "With the three of us stashed away where Ripoll can't find us, we contact him; we call him up and we level with him. We tell him that it was a mistake, that we bit off more than we could chew and that, in return for our safety and our families' safety, we'll transfer the money back to his Swiss account."

"But once he has it," Dourian said, "what's to stop him coming after us?"

"Because he won't be getting it all at once. The deal is we release, say, six million dollars of that money to him every year for the next twenty-five years. And we make it clear that if anything happens to any of us the balance of the money disappears."

Dourian's face softened and lost its frown. "That's not bad, Barney." He looked at Amanda. "That's pretty smart."

"So, in effect," Barney went on, "we'll be asking Ripoll if it's worth all those millions to see us dead. And I can't believe that even a maniac like him would want revenge at those rates."

He looked at Loder, who he knew would be chewing it over, checking it for loopholes. Loder bought it but with reservations. "It'd have to be done properly. You'd have to leave a letter of instruction with a lawyer and let the bank in Bronxville know that you might be in touch with them by mail. We couldn't afford to bluff on this thing because you can just bet Ripoll's going to try and find a way of getting around it, and he'll check it out for a start."

"You're right," Barney said. "If we do it for real, it gives it a better chance of working. But there's also another point to be considered."

Loder supplied it. "The chance that it doesn't work. That he doesn't go for the deal."

"He'll go for it," Dourian said. "He'll have no choice."

"All the same, we still need a contingency plan to fall back on just in case he doesn't," Barney said. "In which case, we'll only have one thing left to us. We'll be forced to fight."

Dourian didn't believe him. "Take on twenty-five hoods? Us?"

"You're not serious," Amanda said.

"Not just by ourselves, no," Barney admitted. "We've got money, we'd get help."

"I don't like it, Barney," Loder said. "Once you go to the Mob they own you for life."

"I'm not thinking about that kind of help. Listen." Barney leaned forward and explained. "What we'd be up against is, in fact, a small private army. Now I'm no expert on these things,

105

but I'm pretty sure that one army can beat another bigger than itself if the conditions are right—better leadership, better equipment, that kind of thing. What I'm suggesting is that it may be possible, given the right weapons and expert guidance, for the three of us to become a better army than the Pachones."

Dourian and Loder just stared back at him, but Amanda spoke. "That's what you were talking about when you said I couldn't help?"

"I just don't see you with a rifle, Amanda."

"I don't see myself with a rifle," Dourian said. "Honestly, Barney, that's the wildest thing I ever heard. I don't know one end of a gun from the other. And I'll bet Tom doesn't, either."

Loder confirmed it. "I went rabbit hunting once when I was a kid, and that's it."

"I know all that," Barney answered. "I don't know anything about guns, either. But what if we got a guy who did? Somebody who could get us whatever we needed?"

Dourian had trouble with it. "Say this guy could get us bigger and better guns than the Pachones have. They're no good to us if we can't use them."

"We can learn to use them. The guy could teach us. Look, we've got eight or nine days. Can you move your vacation up?"

"Sure, if it'll help."

"Tom?"

"No problem."

"Then this is what I suggest. We see a lawyer

and make the arrangements we talked about. We take our vacations now, move ourselves out of here, and move the two families to another part of the lake. But first of all, like tomorrow, we have a try at finding somebody who can help us if it comes to a fight. Now that's what I suggest; so what do you think? Amanda?"

"I think the first part's fine. I just wish the last part included me."

"Don't worry about it. George?"

"Well, it's a plan of action, and it seems to be the only one. So I've got to be for it."

"That leaves you, Tom."

"I agree that we have to try to protect ourselves. I'm just wondering where we're going to start looking for this gun expert."

Barney had the answer all wrapped up and ready to go. "How about that computer of yours? You keep files on army brass?"

"Well, sure, they're good administrators." He saw what Barney was getting at. "That's not a bad idea. An ex–army man."

Taking his plan as accepted and the meeting over, Barney stood up. The sun had shifted across the sky and they were losing their shade. It winked in bright flashes on a tin bucket that lay in the sandbox Loder had made for his children. Next to the bucket was a rag doll, the stuffing coming out of it, the little dress torn. Barney wrenched his eyes away and furiously shut out the analogy that tried to sneak into his brain.

He swapped a few more words with the group, arranged something with Loder, then went back to his own garden.

There was a sandbox there, too. His children's. But he didn't look at it. Instead he grabbed hold of the mower and finished cutting the grass.

Chapter Eleven

Barney told the first officer Loder came up with, a major working for an electronics firm, that he was a writer and wanted to talk to a weapons expert who trained men in their use. The major told him that what he wanted was a drill sergeant, a D.I. as they called them now, and put him onto a lieutenant he thought could probably find him one. Barney expanded his story for the lieutenant, telling him that he also wanted to talk to somebody who'd spent some time in a military prison. The angle was, he said, to find out how they adjusted to civilian life afterward. Barney figured that somebody who'd been inside might know something about getting hold of military equipment and might be willing to part with the information for a price. The lieutenant told him that his best bet was to contact one of the military prisons and quickly got onto the subject of his first request, the D.I.

He gave him the name of a sergeant who had a desk job in an army recruitment center on lower Broadway, and Barney called him and arranged to buy him lunch. He was very pleasantly surprised when the sergeant, a large man running to fat, solved both his problems at the same time.

"You want a guy who lives around the New York area, I guess."

"That would be preferable," Barney replied. They were eating Osso Bucco and drinking beer with it. The man forked up a mouthful, chewed noisily, and spoke through it.

"You wanna talk to Jack Gonella. What he doesn't know about weapons ain't worth knowing."

"Gonella," Barney repeated. "A lot of experience, huh?"

"Oh, sure. Used to be over at Leonard Wood. The D.I.s have a kind of competition going with the rookies, the recruits, you know? See who can shape 'em up fastest. Well, sir, Gonella's platoon always won. Didn't matter what he got—farm boy, stockbroker—didn't matter to him. He'd lick 'em into shape so fast you wouldn't believe."

"This man Gonella, do you know what he's doing now? Can I reach him?"

"Lives in Staten Island. Got a piece of a health club over there. I could dig his address out of records."

"That'd be swell of you. He sounds like the guy I'm after."

The sergeant reached for his beer, gulped half of it down, and wiped his hand over his mouth.

"That other thing you want, guys who been in the slammer, I can't help you much there."

"You ever known anybody who was convicted?"

"A couple, sure, but nobody real well. Excepting Ray Cambell, but you don't want him."

"Why not?"

"He's a bad ass."

Barney pressed him. "You served with this man Cambell?"

"Oh, sure. He was a D.I., too."

"No kidding. Here, let me top that off." He poured beer into the man's glass and waved at the waiter for another bottle. "He was a drill sergeant?"

"And then some. He knew more'n anybody."

"More than the guy you were telling me about —Gonella?"

"He trained Gonella. He trained all the D.I.s down at Jackson there."

"Jackson?"

"Fort Jackson, South Carolina. They run a big D.I. school there. Cambell was the chief instructor."

"He must know his business," Barney said, watching the waiter arrive with the beer. The waiter dumped half the bottle into the sergeant's glass, then hurried away. The fat man drank into the foam, his head nodding at Barney's statement.

"That guy," he said, "I tell you. When I was at Jackson, Cambell was there, too. We used to share BT, basic training, him and me and a

111

couple of other noncoms. Thing was, we were supposed to take these recruits for a mile run before chow. One man, six o'clock in the morning, and a hundred and fifty of these hungry bastards freezing their asses off. You'd turn 'em left and double 'em off. But when they got to the first cross street, they'd wheel into it, double back and into chow. Took no notice of you. Run right over you, you got in their way. But you know something, when it was Cambell's hitch, they went every fuckin' step of the way. *Then* they had chow."

"What, did he threaten to beat up the first man who turned, something like that?"

"Nah. Plenty guys bigger'n him. It's just like, one guy tells you to do something you give him an argument. Another guy tells you to do something, you do it."

"What got him into trouble?"

"They caught him with his hand in company stores."

"Guns?"

"What else?"

Barney asked about his sentence.

"A lot of months making little rocks out of big ones, then a DD."

"Is that some kind——"

"Dishonorable discharge."

"What happened to him then?"

The sergeant took another pull at his glass, then made a face. "There's not a whole lot can happen to you with a DD. You're a felon, who's going to hire you? You can't never be bonded, can't travel, you can't even vote. You get one of those numbers you know it."

"What's he doing now?"

"Loading a truck, sweeping the streets, who knows?"

"Around town?"

"Boston, Philly, somewhere in the East as I recall." The sergeant looked at Barney sharply as if he'd just become aware of Barney's interest in the man.

"But I'm giving you advice. Stay away from Cambell."

"Why?"

The soldier was irritated. "Like I said, he's a bad ass."

When Barney got back from lunch, he called the lieutenant he'd spoken to earlier, who got Cambell's address for him. Then he got busy on a new cabin for the two families. He had his secretary call a realtor in Lake George; there was a cabin vacant in Diamond Point, across the lake from where they were staying at Kattskill Bay. It cost the earth, but Barney took it. He called his wife and explained about the switch telling her he was getting a much better deal on this other cabin but that the owner wanted to keep it quiet. She wasn't to tell her friends or anybody about the move.

Just before quitting time he made two more phone calls, the first to the manager of the Bronxville bank. He identified himself as Steven MacDonald and told him that if he were to receive written instructions from him regarding the disposition of his bank balance, he was to act upon them without question. The manager said he understood. The second call was to his lawyer. Without going into any details, he told him he'd run into a spot of bother and that, just as a precaution, he was sending him a letter that was to be mailed to the manager of the Stuyvesant State Bank in Bronxville if anything untoward should happen to him.

He left the office just before six and bought a street guide to Newark, which was where Cambell lived. He had a couple of drinks and some ribs at a steak house, got a cab to the Port Authority and a bus to Newark. It was a trip he'd made a number of times and it never got any better for him: the sour refinery smell, the long strip of highway, the pointless expanse of the Meadows, the descending planes dragging fumes through the sky—he'd always thought it a dreary introduction to mainland America.

Cambell didn't live far from the bus station and Barney walked there. The houses on the street were of identical brick and wood frame badly in need of paint, the gates rusty and leaning, the fences kicked in. Most of the cars parked at the curb were five or six years old, broken now and then by a brand-new Impala or LTD, their owners apparently preferring to spend their money on transportation rather than rent.

Barney checked the numbers of the houses against the address he had and went up the

114

steps of the one he was after. There were four
rusted tin mailboxes at the doorway, the name
slots on all of them vacant. He knocked on the
first door and was told by a rumpled-looking
woman that Cambell lived upstairs. There were
two doors, and when he saw the man who
opened the first one he knew he wouldn't be
trying the other. Barney had expected him to be
bigger than he was, although the man had good
height and was solid through the chest and
shoulders and had a flat stomach. But his physical presence added inches to him. There was no
belligerence in his stance—one hand holding the
door open, the other loosely by his side—yet
Barney got the impression that it would have
taken three men to get by him. The face matched
that impression; the nose was fine and dead
straight, the mouth well shaped, strength in the
jaw, firm. His eyes were pale with crow's feet
in the corners, the result of a permanent squint.
He looked at Barney as if a bright light was
shining behind him in the hall.

"Ray Cambell?"

"That's right."

"My name's Rivers. Can I talk to you for a
moment?"

"What about?" The voice was deep, the words
said with slow emphasis, as if he were making
sure you heard him the first time.

"Money."

The lines around the man's eyes deepened
fractionally. "I don't owe you money, mister."

"That's true. But I could owe you some."

"What's on your mind?"

"I have a proposition for you. But I'm not going to talk about it out here in the hall."

The pale eyes checked him over, taking their time, then the man stepped back. Barney walked forward, Cambell closed the door and turned.

"All right, let's have it."

"It's going to take a few minutes. Can we sit down?"

Cambell held his gaze for a moment then moved into the room and Barney followed. It wasn't a long walk; the room was small. There were three brown cane chairs topped with faded cushions, a low table on a rug colorless with wear, and two lamps, the shades both showing burn marks. There was another room, and in the corner a small gas ring and a utility refrigerator. Barney took one of the chairs; Cambell remained standing. Looking at him now, Barney saw that he was younger than he first thought; forty maybe. He also saw that he was waiting for an explanation.

"I got involved in a project that turned sour and landed me in big trouble. Me and two friends of mine. There's a man who's going to be after our heads very shortly. We're pretty sure we can buy him off, but there's no guarantee. And if we can't we'll have to take him on. None of us owns guns or knows the first thing about them. We need a man who's not only an expert and can teach us quickly but someone who can get us guns, too."

"Who are you?"

"I told you, my name's Rivers. I live up near Tarrytown. I dipped into a man's Swiss bank account and he turned out to have friends."

"Who gave you my name?"

"A sergeant I talked to. He remembered you from Fort Jackson. His name's Larsen."

Cambell absorbed the information. "Did Larsen tell you I could get you guns?"

"No, he didn't. And if you can't, tell me now and I'll get out of here."

"Good-bye," Cambell said.

"Look, we need help badly. If you can't get us guns, we'll get them from somewhere else. But you could train us, show us how to use them. You can name your own price." As he said it, Barney pulled a wad of ten-dollar bills from his pocket and tossed it onto the table. It was the right move. Cambell only glanced at it, but he saw it, all right.

"You say there's three of you?"

"Three."

"How many of them?"

"Twenty-five."

The only reaction from Cambell was a barely perceptible sideways shake of his head.

"Save your money, mister."

"I know they're long odds, but answer me this: Isn't it possible, given the latest army equipment, isn't it possible for three men to hold off a much larger force who just have regular guns?"

"Maybe. If the three men were weapons experts with combat experience."

"But if they weren't. If they were just three

guys who'd learned in a hurry but could choose the time and place, who had time to get set up. Wouldn't that be possible?"

"You're talking about amateurs outnumbered eight to one. You know what odds the army works with? With professionals? Three to one going *for* you. If you don't have those kind of odds, you stay out of a fight."

"Sure, but you're talking about two armies that are fairly evenly matched in equipment. I'm talking about two groups in which there's no comparison in equipment. And that has to alter the odds."

"No," Cambell said. "You have to figure in casualties on those odds. Say you got lucky and you took out five or six of them. But you lose a man, too. Now it's two against nineteen. The odds have lengthened on you." He paused, thinking about something. Barney could see he wasn't swaying him with his argument—his best argument was lying on the table—but he got the feeling that Cambell saw something else in the situation, perhaps the academic exercise it offered.

"These men. What do you know about them?"

"They're bodyguards of the man whose money I stole. His name's Ripoll. They're all vicious killers."

"You seen them?"

"All but one of them. And then only for a few minutes."

"How did they impress you?"

"Real pros. They work as a team and they're very slick."

"What were they wearing?"

"Ordinary summer clothes. Slacks and jackets."

"The jackets buttoned?"

Barney thought about it. "Yes, I think they were. Except for two of them covering Ripoll from a balcony. They just wore slacks and shirts."

"A balcony. Did they come out onto it or stay near the doors?"

"I remember noticing that. They stayed near the curtains on either side."

"Anything else?"

"They ride in four big black Cadillacs. Heavy looking, low down on their suspension. Green-tinted windows."

"Okay," Cambell said. "The men on the street were wearing shoulder holsters, which means a heavy gun, automatics or thirty-eights. The men on the balcony were standing next to rifles. What about the man you didn't see?"

Barney gritted his teeth and swallowed as a picture flashed into his memory. "He carries a knife. I know that for sure."

"Forget about knives. You let any of those men close enough to use one, you'd be dead anyway. Your problem is twenty-two handguns and two rifles. And four armored Cadillacs. You told me you were in big trouble. . . ."

"Yes. . . ?"

"You're right."

Cambell had only just heard about the Pachones, but he already knew more about them than Barney. Barney was impressed but didn't say so; he said nothing, figuring that if he kept quiet Cambell might just talk himself into it.

"You think you could make them come to you?"

"I can guarantee it."

"So you could choose the terrain and the defensive position. . . ."

"Absolutely."

"How long before they come?"

"About a week."

Cambell looked at him as if he were joking. "Mister, it takes that long just to get a new recruit out of bed in the morning. You reckon on seven weeks to turn a man into a soldier, and that's working with a twenty year old who isn't way out of shape."

"We don't need the full course, Cambell. Just somebody to show us how to load and fire a rifle and maybe hit something with it. And a week's got to be enough because that's all the time we've got."

"It's way too short."

Barney could feel the man getting away from him and switched to a more persuasive argument.

"What do you make a week? What's your time worth to you?"

"These days, not a hell of a lot."

"I'll pay you two thousand dollars and take care of all the expenses." Barney went to his jacket again and laid hundred-dollar bills on the table. "There's half right now. And I'll pay you an extra five hundred for the name of somebody who can get me guns."

This time, when Cambell looked at the money, his eyes stayed on it. He seemed to wait forever before saying quietly, "I can get you guns."

Barney breathed an inward sigh. If Cambell had let him down on that score, he wouldn't have known where to go.

"All right, the five hundred's still yours. And I'll match it again on top of whatever they cost."

He pulled a business card from his wallet, took out a pen, and scribbled his address on it. He asked the other man if he owned a car and Cambell said that he could rent one.

"This is where I live. Come over around ten in the morning. Can you get away that fast?"

"No problem."

"Fine. We'll drive upstate and pick out a spot where nobody'll bug us."

Barney stood and Cambell picked up a bundle of money, seemed to weigh it in his hand, and tossed it back again.

"You know what you're buying, don't you? A half-baked education."

"No," Barney said. He moved toward the door. "What I'm buying is simply insurance."

Chapter Twelve

By ten o'clock that morning they'd closed up their houses, packed their bags, and were ready to go. Amanda had been the only problem; she hadn't been crazy about going up to the cabin and just waiting there, wondering what was happening; she had fussed and protested but, in the end, had reluctantly given in. Dourian had driven her into Tarrytown and put her on a bus for Albany and Lake George. They could have dropped her off themselves since they were going within a few miles of the cabin, but Dourian didn't want her to meet Cambell; Cambell meant guns, and he didn't want Amanda to have anything to do with that side of it. In fact, he'd resisted the whole idea of Cambell when Barney had got back and told them about the man he'd hired. Cambell sounded fine to Tom Loder but it wasn't hard to see why Dourian had gone cold on the idea: He didn't want to be parted from

Amanda. So when he got back from Tarrytown, he was in a rotten mood and resentful of Cambell before he'd even met him. And Cambell's cold terseness didn't do anything to help matters. Nor did his reaction to Dourian's clothes.

He arrived at ten thirty driving a Chevrolet van, and Barney made the introductions. There were no handshakes, Cambell not being the type that inspired contact. He ran his eyes over Loder and Dourian, checking out the new material. Loder was dressed in much the same way as Barney, a polo shirt, suntans, and slip-ons. Dourian, however, was wearing a vest over a tie-dyed shirt, flared chinos, and sneakers. Cambell surprised him by asking if he had any boots.

"What?"

"Boots," Cambell said.

Dourian looked sour. "No, I don't have any boots. What the hell are we talking about boots for?"

Cambell left his eyes on him for a moment, then asked the other two men the same question. He got the same answer but phrased more politely. Cambell nodded at their bags.

"What's in those?"

"Clothes," Barney replied.

"Leave them here."

"Aw, come on," Dourian said. "We're going for a whole goddamn week. I need a change of clothes."

Cambell eyed Dourian's outfit again. "Mister, you sure do."

Dourian was about to take it further, but Barney killed it quickly by picking up a bag and thrusting it into Dourian's arms. They put the bags in Barney's house and rejoined Cambell, who was waiting in the van. Barney sat next to him, Loder, and a glowering Dourian sat in back.

They drove to the Tappan Zee Bridge, crossed the river, and stayed on the Thruway. Cambell moved into the right-hand lane and cruised at a steady fifty, which brought a complaint from Dourian.

"Hey, if we're going to the lake, let's get there, okay?"

Their speed remained the same. Cambell said, more for Barney and Loder's benefit than Dourian's, "I don't want to risk being stopped. A cop might just decide to look in back there."

Barney's head swiveled. "You got guns for us? Already?"

"One rifle."

Dourian snickered. "Great. We'll take turns."

Barney turned and gave him a "cool it" look, but Dourian waved it away.

Loder, trying to help, spoke up. "That's pretty fast work. Where did you——"

He stopped himself.

"A gun store. I had a friend buy it for me this morning. It's used but it's been used well."

"If it's store bought," Dourian said, "why are you afraid of the cops?"

Cambell glanced at him in the rearview mir-

125

ror. He had a way of looking at somebody as if he were administering a punishment. "You got a license to own a firearm in this state?"

"No."

"Neither have I."

Barney knew he'd have to have a few words with Dourian, and soon if there wasn't going to be a major blowup. He'd also have to explain about a dishonorable discharge and how it was designed to flatten a man. Barney was pretty sure the only license Cambell would be eligible for was the driver's license he'd used to rent the van, and even that he would have had to reapply for. But there was no more trouble just then. Dourian maintained a surly quiet and everybody else settled for watching the efficient dullness of the Thruway. Barney wondered if he were kidding himself that three Westchester commuters could ever really expect to be a match for a group of killers. Tom Loder, he knew, had his doubts. Cambell sure as hell didn't think so; it was clear that he didn't like the idea of the exercise any more than Dourian did. In fact, Dourian had been saying all morning that Cambell wouldn't arrive; that Barney had been crazy to pay somebody in advance. But Barney thought different; Cambell had struck him as the type who would do what he'd agreed to do, and do it the best he knew how, although Barney admitted he could have been proved wrong.

They made the outskirts of Albany in a little under three hours, paid the toll at the Northway exit, and followed Eighty-seven north. They drove through pretty country, through Saratoga Springs and Glen Falls, the Adirondacks rising now, pines appearing, and took the turnoff to Lake George. The town itself was situated at the southern tip of the lake, and the lake was a spectacular sight. The water reflected a cloudless sky, stretching away in a brilliant blue and backdropped by high mountains that brought their forests tumbling down to the water's edge. The scene would have looked at home on a postcard from Switzerland. "It never fails to surprise me," Barney said.

The remark wasn't addressed to anybody in particular, but it was completely lost on Cambell. He was more interested in the shops of the little town. He pulled the van over and slid it into a parking slot in front of a general store. It was a big, rambling place, canoes propped up against the doors, rubber floats and water-sports equipment piled up opposite. There was a dummy standing in the window decked out in fishing gear and behind it a huge assortment of rods and reels and lures. Pushed to the back of the window was a display of shotguns.

Tom Loder drew an obvious conclusion. "We buying ammo here?"

"Boots," Cambell answered.

That got Dourian started again. "What do you have, a foot fetish? What's wrong with the sneakers I'm wearing?"

Cambell turned in his seat. "Are you here to learn guns or tennis?"

While Dourian was thinking of an answer,

Cambell climbed out of the van and went into the store.

"Jesus, that guy!" Dourian said through his teeth. "Does he think I'm going to pull the trigger with my toes?"

"Look," Barney began. "Take it easy, huh? Stop needling him; it's not going to help."

"Good advice, George," Loder said. "I've got a feeling about this guy. I wouldn't push him."

"I'll push his friggin' head in if he starts on me again."

Barney tried to soothe him. "George, we've got to get through a week with the man. What do you say you have a try at getting along?"

Dourian blew out a breath that seemed to let out a lot of steam, too. "Okay," he said. "But I'll tell you, Barney, when you picked Cambell you sure picked a surly one."

"Just as long as I picked a good one." Barney got out and the other two followed him into the store. Cambell was walking around checking over the merchandise, and Barney asked him what kind of boots they should buy.

"The best they have. And make sure they fit properly. You'll need polish for them, too."

"Polish?" Dourian said.

Barney shot him a warning look as Cambell continued.

"Six pairs of socks each. And some heavy denim pants and a couple of strong work shirts."

It took half an hour to outfit the three of them, and Cambell made them change into the clothes there and then and had their old clothes wrapped. Standing looking at himself in front of a mirror, Dourian took in the plain twill shirt, the old style, heavy-starched jeans, and the shiny boots.

"Will you look at me?" he invited. "I look like a hog farmer."

They walked out, stiff in their new clothes, and waited while Barney went off to a real estate office a few doors down. They didn't have anything close to what he was after but recommended another place. It was at the other end of the main street and they drove there.

The man behind the desk looked as if he might have been the original realtor, an old man long since gone into and come out of retirement. "I've got a real toughie for you," Barney told him. "I only want a place for a week, but it's got to be really isolated. My son has a rock group, strictly amateur, but they sure make as much noise as anybody. So it has to be way off where we won't disturb anyone."

"A week," the old man said. "Kind of tough right now, it being the season an' all, but I do have one place, up near Brant Lake. Family supposed to take it all summer, then up and left on me. I'd really like to rent it through Labor Day, but I guess you could have it for a week. Sleeps six."

"Fine. I'd like to take a look."

"It's a real nice place, but it'd work out kind of expensive just for a week."

The old man half closed his eyes and riffled through his memory. "Only other place I've got that's off by itself is a place I own. Out at Little Bear Lake. Bought it from Frank Cooper years ago. It's nothing fancy. Got an old Ford engine runs a generator, you cook on butane, and the plumbing's out back. But it's clean, and if you're on a budget it might suit."

"No neighbors?"

"Coon and deer's about all. No folks for miles."

He produced a map of the area and marked in the locations of both cabins, handed Barney the keys, and told him to take a look and let him know what he thought. Barney went out to the van and they started north.

They only had twenty miles to go to the first place, a very large and fairly new A frame almost buried in pines. Inside was a big stone fireplace, exposed beams, hooked rugs, and solid, comfortable furniture. It was right on the lake and there was a jetty and a ski boat that went with the rental. Dourian felt better the moment he saw the house and admitted that if he had to he could spend a week there.

The interior was the last thing Cambell looked at. He spent the main part of his time walking around the property, moving to one end of the entrance road and looking back at the cabin, then doing the same in reverse. When he did go inside, it was only to check on the view from the windows.

They locked up the house and followed the map to the second place. It took them around in a semicircle to Highway Twenty-eight. There was an old tin sign five minutes farther on that said "LITTLE BEAR LAKE" in peeled lettering, and the road to it, unpaved and full of potholes, snaked through the pines for a slow, bumpy two miles. It finally came to a broken-down fence, then looped a clump of pines and joined itself again. Beyond the fence was a clearing, a rutted grass stretch that sloped up to a small pine cabin. A hundred yards behind it, a newer house had been built at the foot of a rocky cliff that went up sheer for a way, then straggled off into the tree-covered hills. The clearing was bordered by two thick clumps of pines that ran from the cliff down to the road. On the left side the pines gave onto a scrubby lake, an ugly expanse of water with rocks breaking its surface and reeds instead of a beach.

Barney led the way to the little cabin. It proved to be three rooms—a tiny kitchen, a bedroom with an iron bedframe and a mattress rolled up on it, and a small living room. Whoever had built the main cabin had taken the little one as a model; it was the same, only a lot bigger and with a few more comforts. The main room had a big stone fireplace and some nicely carved rockers in front of it. Next to that was the kitchen, then a bedroom with two double bunks and some chairs. There was a door in the end wall that led outside. As the old man had said, it was clean but it was also bleak, cold in the shadow of the cliff, and there was a musty, closed-up smell in the air.

Dourian wrinkled his nose as he looked around him. "This is the one. This is the one he'll pick."

Outside, Cambell was standing between the two cabins, hands on hips, taking a long time looking the place over. He walked around the perimeter, disappeared into the pines, and surfaced again on the other side. Then he came into the cabin and looked back at the slope through the windows.

"This one," he said to Barney.

Dourian grunted, disgusted. "What did I tell you."

Cambell ignored the remark, told them to get settled in, and left. They divided the chores. Loder and Dourian got the cabin working while Barney drove back to Lake George to pay the agent. Cambell went with him and made him stop at the store again, where he bought a gallon of paint and some brushes. Then he made a phone call while Barney picked up some groceries, and they headed back.

They left the van at the broken fence and walked up the slope, Cambell going into the little cabin while Barney walked on to the main cabin with the box of groceries. Dourian met him at the door, took them from him and started unpacking.

"Barney, you cretin." He emptied the box in a hurry. "You forgot the booze."

Barney gave him a sheepish grin. "I didn't forget it. Cambell wouldn't let me buy any."

The tight rein that Dourian had been keeping on himself stretched and snapped. "God-damn it!" he exploded. "What's he think he is, a den mother? He tells us what to wear, he tells us where to stay, and now he's telling us what to drink. Where is he? I want to talk to that guy."

Barney tried to calm him but only fueled the fire.

"Take it easy, George, he's not here. He's making up the little cabin."

"He's going to sleep down there?"

"So he says."

"Why? Does he think he's going to catch something bunking with us?"

"George," Loder said, trying to sound like the voice of reason, "you're forgetting something. We hired Cambell as a teacher, to tell us what to do. You can't expect him to be one of the boys."

Dourian snorted. "One of the girls, more likely. All that strong, silent machismo bit. The guy's probably as bent as a nail."

He turned to see Cambell standing in the doorway, looking at him. There was a short heavy silence, then Cambell shifted his gaze to Barney.

"I'm bunking in the cabin. I'll chow down there, too. I'll see you gentlemen at six thirty in the morning."

"Not me, you won't," Dourian said. "I never get up till seven thirty."

Cambell's eyes came back to him and the squint deepened as he walked up to Dourian and stood squarely in front of him. He said slowly and very definitely, "Then you'll have to learn to get your hand off your cock an hour earlier." It wasn't much of an insult but it was all the excuse Dourian needed. He took a fast step forward and swung for Cambell's jaw. It was a good punch, with a lot of shoulder behind it, but it never landed. Cambell swayed back, brought both hands flashing up, and blocked the blow. Dourian gave a grunt of pain as his arm was twisted behind him. He ended up doubled over, his arm stiff, his wrist bent back on itself as Cambell effortlessly held him immobile. Ignoring him, Cambell spoke in his usual deliberate manner to the two other men, who stood rooted in surprise.

"We won't be going into any unarmed combat training, but seeing we have a volunteer here, remember, when you have your man in this position you have two alternatives. You can pull him closer and bring your knee up into his face—the bridge of the nose is a good spot—or if you really want to make sure of him, you can take him down . . ." he twisted his hand slightly and Dourian was forced to step forward and trip over the foot that Cambell put in his way. He sprawled onto his stomach, Cambell moving with him so that the wrist lock stayed as tight as ever . . . "and stamp your heel into the base of his spine."

He relaxed his grip and tossed Dourian's wrist aside as if he were discarding a paper wrapper. He moved to the door.

"Naturally," he said; "that isn't so effective if you're wearing sneakers." Then he left the cabin.

Dourian stayed where he was on the floor. Even though his punch had been useless, just throwing it seemed to have gotten rid of all the steam he'd built up. He lay there massaging his wrist, no longer angry but very embarrassed.

"Well," he said. He looked up at the other two. "I guess he'll think twice before he messes with *me* again."

Chapter Thirteen
Day One

The gunfire woke them, three shots very loud and close by.

"Wazzat?" Loder mumbled. He raised himself on one elbow as Dourian, in the bunk above him, muttered something and turned over. Across the room on the bottom bunk Barney rubbed at his eyes.

"Gotta be Cambell." He lifted a hand to his face and focused on his watch. "Six twenty. May as well get up now."

When Cambell came in ten minutes later, everybody was snoring again. "On your feet. Let's go." He kicked Barney's bunk. "Come on, Rivers, up and out of there." The other bunk got the same treatment. "Snap it up. You've got thirty minutes to be outside." He clumped out of the cabin leaving three very startled men sitting up and blinking.

"I think I prefer the gunfire," Loder said.

They stumbled around in their underwear, went outside, and washed up in icy cold water. There was no bath, and the toilet was an outhouse off in the trees. The cold water did a lot to get rid of the cobwebs, but without coffee they weren't really fully awake when they filed out of the cabin's front door thirty minutes later.

Cambell was waiting for them. "Okay. Tomorrow the same but with a lot more snap. And tomorrow morning you shave your faces and you shine your boots."

"But they're brand new," Dourian said.

"You'll shine them anyway. And you'll dress properly. Tuck your shirt in. You, too, Rivers. Loder, button your sleeve. You start looking sloppy, you'll start acting sloppy."

He watched them critically while they fixed themselves and they watched him back, noting that he certainly practiced what he preached. He wore a heavy cotton shirt, old but better-pressed than their new ones, and stiffly creased cotton pants. His boots glowed with a deep luster. But it was the hat on his head that grabbed their attention; it had a wide, round, dead straight brim, the crown rising and tenting at the top, four indentations on either side—the old-style doughboy's hat that drill sergeants now wore. It sat low on his head just over his eyes, the chin strap worn behind. It looked completely natural on him; it looked as though he'd always worn it.

Dourian, finished with his shirt, started to ask about breakfast.

"Hey, Cambell, is it all right if——"

"Sergeant."

"What?"

"You'll call me Sergeant. Not Cambell, not Sergeant Cambell, not Sarge. Just Sergeant. Is that clear?"

He waited for a dissenting voice. He didn't hear one.

"Let's get the kinks out. Down to the fence railing and back, double time. Go!"

They obeyed the order without thinking and found themselves jogging over the uneven ground down the slope toward the road. They hadn't gone halfway before their breath started coming in heavy chunks, and by the time they'd reached the fence their chests were heaving painfully.

"Wait up," Lodor said, between gasps. "I gotta rest."

Nobody tried to dissuade him. The three of them leaned against the broken railings, turned around, and were about to sit down when they caught sight of Cambell. He was standing where they'd left him, outside the big cabin, standing very still with his hands on his hips, watching them. Nobody said anything, they just started off up the slope. It was tougher going uphill, especially for Loder who was carrying the most weight. But they made it, although they were in no condition to talk about it when they did.

They flopped down on the grass in front of the cabin and sucked in air. Cambell gave them a minute to recover, then put them through a fast series of calisthenics that had their joints cracking and their muscles on fire. Then he called a halt, told them they had thirty minutes to get some chow, and left them prostrate on the grass, looking like bodies recovered from a train wreck. It was a good five minutes before they dragged themselves into the cabin and did something about breakfast.

When they emerged again, feeling a little better now that they had their breath back and some hot food inside them, Cambell called them down to his cabin and sat them on the grass in front of him. He looked them over and said, "Who was doing all that shooting this morning?"

Surprise opened Barney's face. "Wasn't it you?"

"Sure it was me, and you should be kicked in the head for having to ask. Next time you hear guns going off around here, find out who they belong to." He let the words sink in, then went into the cabin and reappeared carrying a rifle.

"What you heard this morning was some test firing. This is what was being tested." The rifle he held was enormous, long and heavy looking with a massive barrel blued to a deep hue. The stock, highly polished walnut, was beautifully carved and crosshatched on the grip and fore-end. "If it looks like it could sting you, you'd better believe it. It's a four-sixty Weatherby, and it's got more power than any sporting rifle made." He took something from his shirt pocket and held it out. "This is why." The cartridge in his hand was a good two-and-a-half inches long with a double neck on the case. With the sharp-pointed bullet head protruding it looked like a miniature moon rocket.

"That's a five-hundred-grain bullet, the grand-daddy of the magnums. It comes out of this barrel with a muzzle energy of eight thousand foot pounds and traveling at half a mile a second. All of which means it'll go through any-thing. There are three to a clip."

Barney raised his eyebrows. "I don't know anything about it, but I would've thought that up against a couple of dozen men a tommy gun would have been better."

"A tommy gun." Cambell left no doubt that Barney was about a hundred years behind the times. "Well, I'll tell you, I'm working on some-thing like that. But I wanted this piece anyway. It's a tough rifle to fire because of the heavy recoil, but it's got two things going for it." He produced another cartridge from his pocket. It was slightly different from the other one; instead of the bullet being completely encased in bronze, some lead showed at the tip. "This is a soft point, a dumdum. It just has to touch a man, wing him, and it'll shock him out of action. Which makes the rifle effective even if you're no marksman. With the other bullets, the fully jacketed ones, it'll take away a man's protection. It'll go right through a tree and the man standing behind it."

"What if he chooses a big tree?" Dourian asked.

For an answer Cambell told them to follow him. They went back to the big cabin and around to one side of it. He pointed down the slope to the clump of pines where the road looped.

"You see the three trees with the white markings? I painted them this morning. They're your targets. Now watch this, because I'll only show you once."

Cambell knelt down, the rifle held across his body, and produced a clip of bullets. "You insert the magazine, slap it home, pull the bolt all the way back, push it forward, and lock it. You don't have to baby it, a rifle's built to handle." He stretched out onto his stomach. "Spread your legs out, twenty to five's the best position, and dig your toes in. Your body should form a frame for the rifle." He showed them how to sight it and how to hold it into the shoulder. "Get that butt pad jammed in there. If you don't, it could break a bone. You release the safety, sight on your target, take a deep breath, hold it, and squeeze the trigger, don't pull it."

Even though his demonstration had been at the pace of his words, he'd still performed it in one continuous action and they weren't prepared for the sudden detonation when he fired. They'd been expecting a loud, fast bang, but the gun seemed to go off in stages like an explosion, a tremendously loud clap of noise that echoed loudly around the cliff behind them.

Cambell ejected a cartridge, got up and handed the rifle to Loder, who took it reluctantly. He'd seen the way Cambell's shoulder had been jerked back by the recoil. He got down onto his stomach, worked the rifle clumsily, sighted it and pulled the trigger. The rifle roared and punched hard into his shoulder. He winced. He'd obviously expected to miss the target, and he did.

So did Barney, who fired the rifle, wincing all the way through. But Dourian did a lot better. Cambell gave him a new clip and when he fired the first round Cambell told him to fire two more. He handled the rifle with a lot more confidence than the other two, his last shot clipping bark from his target. But his success was dampened by the pounding his shoulder had taken. He got up rubbing at it and passed the rifle back to Cambell.

"Christ, what a weapon," he said. "It's lethal at both ends."

They moved off to inspect the targets and Barney said to Cambell, "I guess if we were any good we wouldn't need this much rifle."

"That's right. The better you are the less you need. There was a man name of Cottar, a Texan. He went to Africa, years ago. He killed rhino, buffalo, hippo, lion, everything but elephant. And all he had was a Winchester Thirty-two. But he knew how to use it." The look that accompanied the remark said that Barney would need a bazooka.

They reached the trees and checked Loder's target first. Like Barney's, it was untouched. The one Dourian had shot at had bark missing on one side. Cambell inspected it.

"High and to the right. You're worrying about the recoil. If you hold the rifle properly, so it becomes part of you, it won't bother you." He handed him the big rifle. Dourian took it, dismay written all over his face.

"I won the cigar?"

"It's all yours. From now on, you're the rifleman of this outfit." Cambell moved past him to the tree he'd shot at. "Somebody was asking about a big tree," he said. In the center of the white-painted patch was a neat, clean hole. They walked around to the back of the pine where there was another hole, a lot larger.

Loder gaped at it. "That tree must be thirty inches through."

"Now you know why we've got the Weatherby," Cambell said. "Dourian, take the rifle back to the cabin and lock it up. We're going shopping."

Driving into Lake George, all three of them wondered why they were going back to town when they'd bought a week's groceries the day before. But they were beginning to learn that Cambell was full of little surprises. And that his little surprises got a lot bigger.

He stopped the van in front of the general store, and they trooped in after him and watched him moving around inspecting things. He took a long time. Finally he picked up a few items and took them to a counter. It was a curious assortment: an iron griddle plate, an apple corer, and a small tent pole.

A clerk came over to help. "Can I wrap those for you?"

Loder was standing with him, the other two off checking fishing gear. Loder picked up the griddle.

"We could use one of these, too."

"Two griddles?" the clerk asked.

"Three dozen," Cambell answered. He picked up the apple corer. "And forty of these."

Loder backed off and drifted over to Barney and Dourian.

"Barney, you know Sergeant Cambell. . . ."

"Do I *know* him?"

"He just ordered three dozen griddle plates and forty apple corers."

The information was good for a few seconds' silence. Then they all went over to see for themselves.

The clerk was smiling widely at Cambell, who was asking him if he had any big cardboard boxes out back.

"How many would you like?"

"Three dozen."

By the time he'd finished his purchases, they included shovels, mattocks, baling wire, rope, groundsheets, work gloves, assorted small tools, electrical tape, electrical wire, and a McCulloch chain saw. They loaded the van and left for camp.

Nobody said anything for a couple of miles, the three of them waiting for somebody else to ask the question and get his head snapped off. Barney, as the leader, knew it was up to him.

"Sergeant," he said, coughing behind his hand and creeping up on the question, "about those apple corers. . . ."

Cambell gave him a hard-eyed challenge. "What about them?"

Barney chickened out. "Handy little devils, aren't they."

Bumping up the rocky road to Little Bear Lake, Cambell took the van through the gap in the fence and drove up to his cabin where they unloaded everything. Then he picked up four of the tent poles and told them to follow him. He led them up the slope about forty yards from the big cabin and over to the line of trees. He stabbed one of the poles into the ground, walked on a diagonal toward the center of the slope, and drove another pole into the ground. Then he went back down the slope a little way, stuck in a third pole, and continued to the trees on the other side where he put the fourth one in place. A string tied to the poles would have made a broken arrowhead pointing toward the big cabin.

He turned to them as they trailed along behind him.

"I have to go see a man. While I'm gone, I want a couple of chores done. I want a ditch dug across the left side and a ditch dug across the right. The poles are your markers. Make the ditches about six inches deep and as wide as the mattock blade. But before you do that, unfold the cardboard boxes and set them up. Rivers and Loder, that's your job. While they're doing that, Dourian, you're unscrewing the handles from the griddle plates."

"The handles from the griddle plates," Dourian repeated, nodding. He had a strange look in his eyes.

"I want one plate put into each box, at the end standing up. Then the boxes filled with the earth from the ditches. I want them full and packed down hard and tight. When you're through, stack them in the pines with a ground sheet over them. Then I want that fence repaired as good as new. Rivers, you and Loder can handle that. Dourian, I want you to get in some practice with the rifle. The ammo's in my cabin. When I get back, I want to see holes in your target like a Swiss cheese." He stopped and looked from face to face. "Okay. Everybody know what they're doing?"

Everybody nodded as if they did.

"Then get with it. I want it all done today."

They watched him stride away, get into the van, and drive off.

"Hey," Dourian said. "We're not really going to fill three dozen supermarket boxes with dirt and griddle plates, are we?"

Barney was wearing a thoughtful frown. "I think he's just trying to keep us busy."

"He's chosen a damn funny way," Loder said. He pointed down the slope. "What do we need a fence for out here?"

"Come on," Barney said. "The sooner we get it done the sooner we'll get the answer to the big question."

"What big question?"

Barney sighed. "What he wants done with the apple corers."

They heard the van bumping over the road a few minutes after they'd put the lights out. The door slammed and there was silence.

They were all exhausted from their chores. It had been a lot tougher than they thought digging the trenches and filling the boxes; it was a lot of ground they'd had to cover. They were just dropping off, when Cambell walked into the room and snapped the light on.

"Any of you hear somebody drive up just now?"

Barney, shielding the light from his eyes, affirmed it for all of them.

"You check on who it was?"

Nobody answered. Cambell stood there, mouth

tightly compressed, pale eyes level. "You don't learn much, do you? You're here because you're expecting men with guns. But when you hear shots, you stay in bed. You hear a car engine and you stay in bed. Keep it up and you'll die in those beds."

"Hold it a second." It was Dourian. "Those men don't even know about us yet. And they wouldn't know where to look for us if they did."

"Don't count on it. Anybody can be found. And you can't tell me the exact hour of the exact day when they will know about you."

Loder joined in. "George has a point, though. It's fifty to one they'll come at all. All this we're going through here is really just a precaution."

"Now, listen," Cambell said, his voice lower, harder. "And listen good. You're hoping they won't come. So am I. But we're going to assume they will come. We're going to assume they wouldn't miss this date for anything. So next time you hear a car outside, check into it. If you hear a twig snap, check into it. You're not up here to learn to tie knots, you're here to learn to stay alive. And you won't learn that if you're dead." He glared at each of them in turn, making sure they got the message, then pointed to the corner behind Dourian's bunk. "What's that, Dourian, your golf clubs?"

Dourian turned and looked at the rifle he'd put into its canvas case and propped against the wall.

"It's the Weatherby."

"What kind of use do you think a rifle is wrapped up like that?"

Exasperated, Dourian said, "I thought you'd want me to keep it clean."

"I also want you to keep it ready." Cambell pulled the rifle from its cover, opened the bolt, and peered down the barrel. "How many rounds you get off today?"

Dourian brought a hand up to his shoulder. "Twenty of the mothers."

"How many hits?"

"Seven."

"Seven," Cambell repeated. "Well, I'll tell you, Dourian, I don't think you like this rifle."

"I hate that rifle. Every time I fire it I get wounded."

"I think you'd like it more if you got to know it better. So I suggest you sleep with it tonight."

"What?"

Cambell jerked back Dourian's bedcovers and dropped the rifle into his arms. "And I mean wrapped around it like it was a hundred-dollar whore." He strode across the room and killed the light. He said on his way through the door, "I'll be by later. If you're not cuddling up to it, watch out."

They heard him clump down the steps.

"The bastard," Dourian said. "The rotten lousy bastard." He threw out a few more expletives, then quieted down. A few minutes later, he said, "You know what?"

"What?" Barney asked sympathetically. It'd be tough to sleep with a rifle.

"It reminds me of my first wife."

Everybody broke up. They were too tired not to.

Chapter Fourteen
Day Two

The morning was a replay of the previous one, with a couple of differences: Whereas the day before they'd suffered the rigors of being rudely awakened, then lining up for the outhouse and washing in icy water, this time they had to shave as well, which was murder without hot water, and shine their still glossy new boots, which was a trick they weren't used to. But the major difference came in the way they descended the steps. The running and the calisthenics of the day before, coupled with a full day of manual labor, had made itself felt in muscles long since relegated to a mere supporting role, and they came out of the cabin very slowly and very painfully. But Cambell ignored that and put them through the same run to the fence and back and a fast round of calisthenics that spread-eagled them on the grass again. He told them that they had thirty minutes to eat and be down at his cabin, then walked away as if he were unconscious of the havoc he'd wreaked.

Dourian rolled over slowly and pushed himself to his knees like a fighter trying to beat the count.

"Barney . . ." he panted for breath . . . "I can't hack it anymore. I'm quitting." Loder, worse off than any of them, seconded it. "Me . . ." he sucked air in great gulps . . . "me, too."

But after they'd recovered and gone in for orange juice and coffee and bacon and eggs and more coffee, the picture had changed. All three of them wanted to quit, but nobody wanted to be the first to suggest it. So, thirty minutes later, they were sitting outside Cambell's cabin wondering what was in the oilcloth bundle lying at his feet.

He looked them over before speaking, as if waiting for one of them to come forward and confess to something. They expected him to comment on their previous day's labors; the two ditches were very much in evidence running across the clearing thirty yards behind them, and the fence, the crossbars all raised and wired to the uprights, was conspicuous in its new condition. They had a pretty good idea Cambell had already inspected them, just as they were sure he'd checked the boxes of earth they'd stacked in the pines. But instead, in the sudden, out-of-the-blue way he had of introducing a new subject, he began talking about guns.

"In 1957 a genius by the name of Eugene

Stoner designed an automatic rifle that was manufactured by the Armalite Division of the Fairchild Engine and Airplane Company. It was called the AR Fifteen. It's now made by Colt as the M Sixteen and it's the standard shoulder weapon of the U.S. Army. It's made in several configurations. Rifle, Carbine, Survival Rifle, Heavy Assault Rifle, Submachine Gun, and a couple of others." He knelt and threw back the flaps of the oilskin at his feet. "This is what the submachine gun looks like."

There were two guns on the sheet, both the same. After the Weatherby they looked like toys. Whereas the big rifle was long and elegant with its blued barrel and beautifully carved stock, these guns were short and squat, not much more than two feet in length with plain dark wood on the buttstock and barrel, the middle section an ugly metal jumble of levers and flanges. The carrying handle on top and the high triangular sight on the barrel tip poked up, while the pistol grip and the magazine in front of the trigger guard jutted down. Together they gave the gun an awkward, ungainly look, as if it couldn't make up its mind what it was supposed to be. Barney said as much. "It sure doesn't look like a submachine gun."

Cambell picked up one of the guns, pressed a lever, and pulled at the buttstock. It telescoped out on twin metal rods, lengthening the weapon.

"It doesn't, huh? It can kill thirty men in two seconds."

155

The three of them took another look at the gun.

"Must fire a pretty big bullet," Dourian suggested.

"Five fifty six millimeter, which is only a hair bigger than a twenty-two."

The information brought a comment from Loder. "When I was a kid, we went after rabbits with a twenty-two. But they'd keep on running unless you hit them in the head."

"The twenty-twos you were using were limping along. This thing's faster than the Weatherby."

"It makes a difference, the speed?"

Cambell changed his grip on the machine gun. "A slug from this will go straight through a man a quarter mile away. That's if you missed bone. If you didn't, you'd get an exit hole the size of a soup plate. All because of the high velocity."

"Does it fight back like the Weatherby?" Predictably, it was Dourian's question.

"Very small recoil. And no kickoff at all." He got a lot of blank looks.

"Kickoff. The upward movement of a gun. If you can reduce the angle of the butt in relation to the barrel, if you can get them in a straight line like this gun, the recoil goes back instead of up and you get a much more accurate weapon."

"Then if it's fast and powerful and deadly, why am I breaking my shoulder with the Weatherby?"

"Because they're going to do different jobs.

Exactly what I'll tell you later." Cambell spoke to them all now. "All right, Twenty Questions is over. Now just shut up and look and listen. Rivers, Loder, these are your guns. I'm going to show you how to run them, how to load, aim, fire, clean, and strip them. You'd better learn quick and you'd better learn good, because we don't have time to go back over it. Dourian, you watch, too. You may have to use one of these things. Okay, step one. Loading. . . ."

He took them through everything, dry firing he called it, and by lunchtime they still hadn't fired a shot. They grabbed a fast bite and started in again and an hour later he let them try the guns for real.

"You first, Rivers. Pick your target and fire when you're ready."

Barney was a lot more nervous than he'd been when he fired the Weatherby. The Weatherby, after all, was only a super-version of the kind of thing you fired in a penny arcade. But this thing he held in his hands now . . . thirty men in two seconds!

"Keep your right hand firm and use your left as a guide. Try and relax, but don't let it get away from you."

Barney knelt as Cambell had showed him, inserted a box magazine into the well, and pushed it upward till the catch engaged. He pulled back the charging handle, pushed it forward again, and thumbed the selective fire button on to Auto. Hugging the gun into him he gripped the barrel with his left hand, curled his other hand around the pistol grip, and sighted on his target. He felt the trigger against the inside of his finger and slowly squeezed down on it.

The gun exploded, danced in his hands and went on dancing as if it were never going to stop. The noise was one long continuous hammering over which he sensed more than heard Cambell shouting at him. The gun stopped as suddenly as it had started, the shots still echoing in his ears.

"Beautiful, Rivers. You got off an entire magazine and all you hit was leaves."

Barney had made the classic first-timer's mistake of keeping the trigger depressed, unconsciously expecting to fire a single shot. Cambell clued him in.

"You have to learn to fire in three- or four-round bursts. A fast squeeze and release. Now try it again, and remember it's a light piece; so you're going to have to control it."

On his second attempt, he got the gun to stay steady, and on his third magazine he was firing in short bursts. One of them made the bark fly on his target.

"I hit it," Barney cried, delighted.

He swung around, the gun still at his waist, his finger still curled around the trigger. As one man, Cambell, Loder, and Dourian dived for the ground.

Barney stopped short. "I'm sorry, I——"

"Rivers." Cambell's voice cut through him.

"Point the gun into the air . . . now move it to Safe. . . ."

When Barney had complied, Cambell got slowly to his feet. He brushed himself off, walked forward close to Barney, then brought his face up level. "Rivers, if you ever turn around on me again with a machine gun in your hands, I'll take it away from you and break it over your head."

Barney's face was white. "I'm sorry, I just——"

"Hold the gun above your head. Both hands."

Barney pushed it into the air.

"Now double down to the fence like that. And back again. Move!"

Barney moved.

"All right, Loder, you're on."

If Tom Loder had been nervous before, he was even more so now. But he had the advantage of going second and learning from Barney's mistakes. Even so, his first burst wasted half the magazine. But when he learned not to be afraid of the gun, his shots started to thump into his target more often than they missed. Then Cambell let Dourian try the gun. Dourian couldn't believe its lightness and its lack of recoil. He was hitting the target while he was still on his first magazine.

"I love it. It's like a popgun after the rifle. Tom, I'll trade you anytime."

"You sure about that?" Cambell asked. "You get caught with the rifle you'll get fined for not having a license. If Loder gets caught with a machine gun he'll go to jail for twenty years. Go get the rifle."

Dourian went off looking like he had a dental appointment. Then Barney came back from his trip to the fence, his arms stretched above him, his legs moving in more of a controlled stumble than a coordinated run and flaked out on the grass. Cambell didn't acknowledge his arrival; instead he yelled at Dourian to hurry it up.

When he came back with the Weatherby, Cambell handed him four clips and told him he wanted to see some good shooting. Dourian reluctantly lowered himself into the prone position and started. His first shot was a miss. And his second and third. Cambell talked to him, gave him pointers, corrected his firing position. He missed only one more time.

"Eight out of twelve," Cambell said. "You call that good shooting?"

Defensively, and also because it was his best score yet, Dourian said, "I thought that was great shooting."

"Great shooting's twelve out of twelve."

"Then I'll settle for good shooting," Dourian answered. "What's good shooting?"

"Also twelve out of twelve."

Cambell told him to go down to his target to see what kind of grouping he'd got and dispatched Loder on the same errand. "On the double!" he called. Then in another of his instant subject switches, he turned to Barney, who was beginning to recover from his own run. "The important part of any combat situation happens before it starts. I'm talking about Intelligence. Ideally, you should know as much about the enemy as he knows himself and keep him from finding out anything about you. As far as you know, how many men will they think they're up against?"

"Just one. Me."

"Then you'll be three times the strength they figure, not that that cuts much ice, seeing how much they outnumber you. But what does count is the way you're armed. They'll figure a hand gun or, at most, a shotgun. So what you're going to have going for you is surprise, and surprise has been winning battles since the weapons were clubs."

Barney nodded, wondering what Cambell was getting around to.

"As far as their armament goes, you can't afford to guess. You have to find out for sure what they've got. Is that going to be possible?"

"I think so. I only have one contact but he knows them pretty well."

"I want to know how they operate, how they're armed, how they kill, the way they work. Twenty-five men is a small army, and all armies have patterns because their leaders have patterns. I want to know what it is."

Barney said he'd go into town and make a phone call that evening. Cambell okayed that and turned to watch Dourian and Loder trotting down the slope toward their targets.

With his back to Barney, he said, "This guy you're going to try to make a deal with—Ripoll.

When do you plan on contacting him? How late can you leave it?"

"Five days at the outside."

When Cambell turned around, he didn't look happy.

Barney said, "We're not shaping up fast enough?"

"You're coming along about like I figured. But I need time to get set up here. And I need weapons, that's the big problem. I can only move as fast as my supplier."

Barney patted his gun. "Well, we're not exactly defenseless."

"You will be if you run out of ammo."

"Is ammo a problem?"

"It's always a problem. When somebody breaks into a National Guard Armory and scoops up a hundred M Sixteens, they don't have much time to take along a zillion rounds."

"Armories? I thought they hit army stores."

"They're starting to. So many armories are getting knocked over that now they're keeping the rifle bolts at police stations."

"Then I guess we're lucky getting what we got."

"We need more. You can't teach a man to use a gun unless he uses it." Cambell nodded at the submachine gun. "And don't let that get you too confident. At the moment, if twenty-five pros arrived out here, they could throw rocks and still beat you."

The words sobered Barney; he'd been under

the impression that two machine guns, plus a rifle that hit like a cannon, was all the firepower they needed to give them an edge. But if that wasn't true, and if there was even some doubt about getting ammunition for what they did have. . . .

For the first time since he'd got there Barney felt the first faint stirrings of unease.

"I want a hole dug," Cambell marked the spot with the heel of his boot, "here. Four feet deep and three feet wide. Rivers, you do it because it's for you."

They'd finished lunch and were standing at the back of Cambell's cabin. After going back to the range, where all three of them had improved on their morning's performance, Cambell had taken them indoors and shown them how to strip and clean their weapons.

Now there was a small grin on Barney's face. "A hole? For me?"

"That's right. And make sure it fits."

The spot Cambell had chosen was a few strides from the rear window of the little cabin.

"Loder, take the chain saw and make that window into a door. Rip it out."

Loder nodded carefully.

"Dourian, I want you to pace off fifty yards and dig a hole for yourself directly in line with the one Rivers digs."

Dourian gave him a bright smile. "Right."

"Loder, when you're through with the window, take a screwdriver and pry off the handles of those apple corers. I'm going into town. I want it all finished when I get back."

He left them with that and strode off down the slope toward the van. They watched him go.

"And he was doing so well," Loder said. "This morning he was all business. Barrel lengths, muzzle velocities, rate of fire. And now, apple corers."

"Doctor Jekyll and Sergeant Hyde," Dourian said.

Loder asked Barney if he had any idea what Cambell was doing.

"No, but I think *he* has. And I think *we'd* better do it."

He set an example by getting a shovel and starting to dig. The others went along, Dourian starting on his excavation and Loder going for the chain saw. When he brought it back, he said, "Barney, this isn't our property and we're wrecking the place."

"I know it." Barney thumped a shovel into the earth. "We'll just have to pay the man."

When they'd finished, they inspected each other's work. Loder had cut through the sill down to the floor, across, and up the other side. He'd removed the window glass and sawn through the frames. What had been a window was now a gaping hole in back of Cambell's cabin. He'd stacked the apple corers in two neat piles, wooden handles on one side and their serrated metal tips on the other.

The hole that Barney had dug looked about the same as the one Dourian had dug farther up the slope. Loder inspected them both and frowned.

"Wait a second, Barney. He told you to dig a hole and he told George to dig a hole. How come I don't get a hole?"

"He's planning to have you cremated," Dourian said.

They'd finished dinner by the time Cambell brought the van back and told them to help him unload. Tied to the roof rack were several sheets of corrugated iron and some quarter-inch plywood boards; these seemed so prosaic after his other purchases that nobody commented. Barney told him that he was going into town to make that phone call and asked if it would be all right if the others came along. Cambell told them to be back in two hours.

It was getting dark when they arrived at Lake George; the sun had sunk behind the mountains and lights were starting to pop on around the lake. Most of the lights in the town itself were shining, including those of a bar a few steps from where they'd parked. They stood on the sidewalk looking at it. Dourian swallowed and ran the back of his hand over his mouth.

"I would kill for a martini. Straight up, no olive, no twist."

"I'll take a double Dewar's on the rocks," Loder said. "Splash of water."

Barney made it two. "With a beer chaser."

They walked up to the window and peered inside. Lights glinted warmly off bottles and soft music floated out to them. The door opened and a man and a woman came out arguing noisily. This snapped them out of it.

"But," Dourian sighed, "I guess Coach Cambell wouldn't like it if we broke training."

The others moodily agreed and they moved down the block to a phone booth and called the cabin at Diamond Point. It was only four miles away on the edge of the lake, but when Barney spoke to his wife he pretended he was calling from Philipse Manor. He told her that Tom and George were over for a drink and were going to make it a party call. He chatted with her about incidentals, talked to the kids, and handed the phone to Loder, who had a similar conversation with his family. Then it was Dourian's turn.

"Hi," Amanda said.

"How are you?"

"Fine."

"They treating you all right up there?"

"Oh, sure. Peggy and Elaine couldn't be nicer and the kids are terrific. But, um. . . ."

"But you miss Macy's."

"I miss *you*, you bastard."

"Listen, I hear they're going to show a profit this quarter."

"George, don't joke. I'm worried about you. I wish you were here or I was there."

"Then we'd both be in different places again."

Amanda knew what he was doing; keeping it light to make it appear that what they were going through was just an elaborate safety precaution. She was grateful for the gesture but it didn't help. She asked in a lower voice, "Nothing's happened yet?"

"Nope, and nothing will. Barney will be calling in a few days; he'll make the deal and I'll come right up and get you."

"Hurry, all right?"

"You can count on it." When Dourian joined them on the sidewalk he looked miserable. "Screw Cambell, I'm going to get a drink."

Barney didn't try to stop him. Instead he went back into the booth and called the restaurant where he'd met Gage. He was lucky, Gage had just walked in.

"Gage? This is Rivers." He left the door open so Lodor could hear.

The voice on the other end was faint. "I can hardly hear you. You sound like you're miles away."

Barney spoke louder. "Sorry, I'm calling from Lake George. Can you hear me any better?"

"A little. What's up?"

"I want to ask you about the Pachones."

"I wish you'd take my advice, Rivers, and forget about Ripoll."

"I may not be able to. Listen, the Pachones, they carry guns, don't they?"

"And they use them. They killed a man Monday."

Barney closed his eyes for a moment; it still seemed incredible to him that something as obscene as the Pachones could be allowed to run around loose.

"Do you know what kind of guns exactly?"

"Rivers, I can tell you their shoe sizes. They carry Colt Troopers, five-inch thirty-eight Specials. All of them except Manolo. You already know what he carries."

"They have rifles as well?"

"Four of them. Remington Seven forty-twos. And Ripoll's personal bodyguard has a sawed-off four-ten pump gun. He never leaves Ripoll's side."

"How about the cars? They bulletproof?"

"Bombproof, too. They're all two-inch armor-plated."

"Gage, when they . . . move against somebody. Any particular time?"

"Always at night. They like the dark."

"One more question. How do you think they'd react if they were up against somebody who gave them a hard time?"

"If Ripoll ordered them to they'd just keep on coming. They'd never question it. Rivers, I don't know what you're planning, but it doesn't sound smart."

Barney told him not to worry, said he'd be in touch, and hung up. He filled Loder in on Gage's replies: "Twenty-four revolvers, four

Remingtons, a shotgun, four bombproof Cadillacs."

"Barney," Loder said, "I'll tell you something. If it comes to a fight, I think you're going to be glad you dug that hole."

They went into the bar, collected Dourian, and drove thoughtfully back to camp.

Chapter Fifteen
Day Three

Their early morning routine changed slightly, but it changed for the worse. After the painful run to the fence and back, and the painful round of exercises, Cambell called a weapons inspection that turned out to be the cause of even more distress. He wasn't satisfied with the condition of Barney's or Loder's weapon and was especially disturbed about Dourian's. He opened the bolt and peered down the barrel.

"What have you got in here, Dourian, a coin collection?"

"Pardon?"

"You get off twelve rounds after I left yesterday?"

"That's right."

"I can see a piece of every one of them in here." He handed the rifle back. "How many hits?"

"Twelve."

Cambell stared at him for a long moment. "I'm going to ask you again, Dourian. You lie to me and I'll double you till you drop. How many hits?"

"Ten. But the other two were close."

"You shouldn't be missing at all. From now on you get twenty-five squat jumps for every one you miss. So you owe me fifty. Outside and start."

For a moment Barney didn't think Dourian was going to do it. He glared back at Cambell as if he were about to give a verbal blast, but he held it in, turned, and clumped angrily out of the cabin. Cambell told Loder to clean his machine gun, told Barney to come with him, and led the way toward the little cabin. They passed Dourian jumping up and down like a frog and swearing.

When they were out of earshot, Barney said, "Cambell. . . ."

"Sergeant."

"All right, Sergeant. Why are you hassling Dourian? Why ride him so hard?"

"I'll tell you why, because he's the top gun, he's got the power. And that makes him the key to what I'm setting up here. He has to learn faster and better than you two. You and Loder will be playing defense but Dourian has to score the touchdowns."

"Okay, but don't push him too far. He's close to picking up and getting out of here."

"His type has to be pushed. I've trained a

hundred Dourians. They're embarrassed to try hard, embarrassed by achievement. But they've got more talent in their little fingers than a dozen gung-ho types. You just have to get it out of them."

Barney wasn't sure that Cambell was right but let it go for the moment and told him what he'd learned from Gage. It didn't seem to faze him, but then you couldn't tell a thing from Cambell's face; as Dourian had remarked, he could be holding a winning lottery ticket or a live scorpion and you wouldn't know which.

They arrived at the hole Barney had dug. Cambell stopped and pointed to the freshly made door in the cabin. "Here's what I want you to do. Go inside to the front window. When you hear the order, I want you to get out of there fast, through that door and into this hole here. You got it?"

Barney said he understood even though he didn't. He'd gotten over being surprised at anything Cambell told him to do; he assumed it was all part of a master plan that would be unveiled when Cambell was good and ready. He stepped up through the door Loder had cut and into Cambell's bedroom. The bunk was made up, the blanket tight, some clothes folded neatly on a chair. Through the door he could see dishes washed and stacked; he was a good housekeeper.

Barney positioned himself at the front window, which was diagonally opposite the door he'd just come through. The window gave onto the grassy slope and was about fifty yards from the fence. He heard Cambell's voice. "Rivers, you ready?"

"Yeah."

"*Go!*"

Barney turned and trotted across the floor, jumped through the door onto the ground, took two strides, and stepped into the hole. He felt pretty silly jumping into a hole, but then, as he told himself, if Cambell had ordered him to jump into Little Bear Lake he would have felt even sillier. But Cambell wasn't amused by Barney's half-hearted effort.

"Rivers, that's the slowest thing I've seen since the horse I drew in the Derby."

"You want it faster?"

"I want it like a blur. I want you coming out of there in a crouch. And when you hit that hole, bury yourself."

Barney climbed out and walked back to the cabin, moved to the front window, and waited for the order. When it came, he shoved himself off the wall, tore across the floor, leaped out of the door, tripped, and fell headfirst into the hole. Stunned, he crawled out, spat dirt, and cleared his eyes.

"Better," Cambell said. He told him to try it again, only this time he was to get out of the hole in a hurry, make a beeline for the pines on his left, and hotfoot it down the trail that ran through the trees to the big cabin. Cambell went back up the slope and stopped at the hole Dourian had dug. He called Dourian over and talked to him for a moment; then Barney saw

174

Dourian step into the hole. Cambell turned and waved a hand and Barney went back into the cabin and waited for the order. From fifty yards away the voice was as clear as a bell.

"Get ready, Rivers. *Go!*"

Barney jumped through the door and, as he made the hole, he got a flash impression of Dourian rising up like a jack-in-the-box, holding his arms as if he were aiming a rifle. And he was aiming at Barney.

Barney scrambled out and scampered for the line of pines, and this time he could clearly see Dourian doing the same as he was doing. He made it to the trail and followed its curving path to the big cabin, where he found Dourian waiting for him. Dourian didn't comment on the exercise and Barney, panting for breath, didn't say anything either. He recognized the symptoms; Dourian was getting progressively quieter, keeping it all in and building up another head of steam.

When they broke for breakfast and then went onto the range, what happened didn't help to cool him down any. Dourian went first. Slowly and methodically, he pumped twelve shots into his target. He looked up at Cambell. "Sorry, it's the best I could do."

The sarcasm wasn't lost on Cambell. "Well, let's see what your best is on rapid."

He changed Dourian's position from prone to kneeling and gave him five seconds to fire each three-round clip. There was just time to work the bolt and take a potshot. Dourian hit on only three out of twelve. Cambell told him what he was doing wrong, and the second go-round he scored five out of twelve but was madder than ever. As he saw it, he'd worked his way up from a hacker to a dead shot and now Cambell had reduced him to a hacker again.

When it was Barney and Loder's turn they had no problem bettering their previous records. Now that they'd started to grasp the technique of firing the machine guns in short bursts, two-thirds of their shots hit home. Late in the morning, Cambell took the van off on another of his mysterious missions and told them to stay on the range and get some practice in. He was back an hour later, just as they were finishing. The first thing he did was check the ammunition box.

"Rivers, you use all the mags that were in here?"

Barney confirmed it.

"Dourian, do you have any rounds left?"

Dourian, rubbing at his shoulder, gave him a surly shake of his head.

Cambell went away and left them wondering why he hadn't checked on their scores. They found out after lunch, when he handed them a couple of surprises and a real bombshell.

"Rivers, that galvanized sheeting you helped unload. I've chalked lines on it. I want it cut on those lines. You'll find metal shears in my cabin."

"Got it."

"Loder, get your chain saw. I want a hole cut in the roof of your cabin. I'll show you where."

"Right," Loder said, as if that was exactly what the cabin needed.

"Dourian. . . ."

Wary and suspicious, Dourian waited.

"Take the van, go into town, and buy three ski masks."

"Ski masks." Sounding almost bored, Dourian said, "That's it. That does it."

"Does what?"

Dourian let him have it. "Ever since we got to this dump, we've been trying to make allowances for the crazy things you've got us doing. You tell us to fill boxes with earth, okay, maybe you've got rubber plants ordered. You buy forty tent poles and forty apple corers, fine, every man should have a hobby. Then you have us jumping in and out of graves. A little macabre, but maybe that's how you get your jollies. But why in the name of freakin' blue blazes do we need three freakin' ski masks?"

In direct contrast to Dourian's long, loud outburst, Cambell's answer was short and quiet.

"Because tonight we're going to pull off a holdup."

Loder said, after the ten-second silence, "I think I'd better sit down for this one."

Dourian wasn't sure whether Cambell was kidding. "You mean it?"

"I just called my supplier, the guy who sells me weapons. He's fresh out of ammo for the machine guns and won't have any more till God knows when. So we're going to have to steal some."

Barney couldn't believe it. "You don't mean knock over an armory?"

"No. A private group."

There was a long pause and a few furtive glances while they checked with each other. Dourian's anger had blown itself out anyway, and now he was as quiet and uncertain as the other two.

Cautiously, Loder said, "What if we offered this group twice what they paid for the ammo? Buying the stuff would be a lot safer than stealing it."

"Agreed. But these people didn't buy it to sell it. We'll have to persuade them to part with it."

"Hold it." Dourian waved a hand. "Hold it a moment. We're out of ammo now, right?"

"Right."

"Then how can we go on a holdup if we're out of ammo?"

"We'll have to go without it." Cambell looked at the startled faces. "My guy can't even get me rounds for the Weatherby, not by tonight. And by tomorrow night that M Sixteen ammo might be long gone."

"It'd be a hell of a bluff," Barney said. "What if they call it?"

"Look, this isn't the Mafia we're going up against, it's a bunch of amateurs. With a couple of choppers pointing at them, they're not going to argue. They're not going to know they're not loaded."

"I'll be honest with you. They'll take one look at my face and they'll know right away they're not loaded."

"That's why I want the masks, so they won't see how nervous you look. And masks will make it scarier for them anyway, which will help."

Nobody had any comeback to that; in fact, nobody made any further comment at all. It was clear that Cambell had made up his mind. They were going on a holdup and they were going tonight, and that was all there was to it.

They got busy on the jobs he'd given them. Barney started on the corrugated sheeting, cutting it along the lines Cambell had drawn. On most of the sheets, the lines were chalked across the ends, but there were some that had three-sided squares on one edge. Just what Cambell wanted them cut for was something Barney didn't bother to think about. He already had his mind full of the job he had to do later that night.

Tom Loder, preoccupied with the same thing, didn't give it a second thought when Cambell had him saw a large hole in the cabin roof next to the chimney.

When Dourian had helped Barney with the iron sheeting for a while, Cambell sent him into town for the ski masks. He was gone about an hour and a half, and when he returned and parked down at the fence, he ambled up the slope toward them as if he didn't really want to get there. When he got closer, Barney saw that

179

he'd fixed his face in an innocent, I-tried-my-best expression. Cambell saw it, too. He held out his hand.

"All right, let's have them. The ski masks."

"Couldn't get any. The guy at the store doesn't get them in till the season starts."

Cambell looked at the paper bag Dourian was holding.

"Then what did you get?"

"I went to three stores," Dourian said.

"You couldn't get masks?"

"Yeah, I got masks. Only they didn't have much choice."

Cambell told him to put one of them on.

"You may not like it."

"Put it on."

Dourian put the bag down, took a cardboard mask from it, and slipped it over his head. Barney and Loder blinked. Facing them was a man with the body of George Dourian and the face of Colonel Sanders, the fried chicken king.

"Aw, George," Loder said. "Come on now."

"It was the only thing they had."

"Couldn't you at least have gotten a stocking?"

Dourian whipped the mask off. "I didn't know your size." He looked at Cambell, waiting for a tirade but it didn't come. Cambell's only comment was to tell Dourian to take some scissors to the masks and enlarge the eyes and mouths.

Two hours later, they stowed the guns in the van and left.

They drove south and picked up the Thruway and sat on fifty miles an hour. Barney asked

Cambell what he knew about the people they were going to rob.

"Some kind of liberation group with initials. Who they're trying to liberate and from what I couldn't tell you."

"If it's not a rude question, how do you know they've got the stuff we're after?"

"Because the guy that sells to me sells to them."

"Not much customer loyalty in the business," Dourian said.

"It's a tough business. And it's getting tougher."

"I would have thought it was a gold mine with all the nut groups around now."

"Sure, but there are a lot of amateurs selling. All those guys back from 'Nam, a lot of them brought machine guns with them."

"They must have a hard time getting them in," Loder said.

Cambell told him that they'd done it legally. "Captured weapons, war trophies. A man would bring in a Chinese AK or a Cong Type Fifty and as long as it was inoperational there was no problem. If it wasn't, the army would simply lead in the barrel or remove the bolt. All the man needed was to find somebody who'd brought back the same kind of weapon with a bolt or a good barrel, whichever he needed. Then they simply made one gun out of two."

Barney grunted. "Simple enough."

"They still need ammo," Cambell added. "It always comes down to that." His comment reminded them of what they'd be facing in a few hours, and there wasn't much conversation the rest of the trip.

The address Cambell was heading for was north of Woodlawn, and they stayed on the Thruway right down to the Cross County Parkway, traveled west on that, then switched to the Bronx River Road. He went half a mile and took a left on a street that led them around the top of the subway railroad yards. He pulled over, checked a road map, went a few more blocks, and parked.

"Three doors down," he said. "Other side."

The house he'd indicated was a dilapidated two-story structure fronted by weather-worn shingles. The screening around the porch was torn and there were three cans of uncollected garbage in the tiny, concrete front yard. On the left, a short narrow driveway ran back to a garage; half way down it an open stairway, partially recessed into the side of the house, led to the top floor.

"We'll give it twenty minutes to see if there's any action, then we'll move. Loder, you wait here behind the wheel. Rivers and Dourian will come with me. We're going up the stairs and in through that door and we're going in hard. There may be two people inside, there may be a dozen, the important thing is to keep those machine guns up and pointing. Both of you cover the area on your side, and I'll take the middle. Set your guns on Auto and get your fingers on those triggers. You've got to look as though you're busting to let fly."

They nodded at the instructions and went back to watching the house. There was a light on upstairs, curtains across the window, a glimpse of somebody moving against them.

The minutes ticked by, the street motionless except for an occasional car. Cambell reached for a door handle. "Loder, be ready to back into that drive and get the doors open. And if you see anything that looks like trouble while we're up there, honk the horn twice."

As he finished speaking, the lights of a small van spilled over them as it swung to a stop in front. A man got out carrying a flat cardboard box and started across the road with it. He had one foot on the bottom step of the house when Cambell caught up with him. "Hey, buddy."

The man turned.

"I'm going up. I'll take it."

The man took a check from his jacket. "Six bucks even."

Cambell gave him the money and a big tip and the man drove off. Cambell ditched the box and waved an arm, and a minute later he was joined by Barney and Dourian. Dourian handed Cambell the Weatherby and the three of them slipped on the masks, then started up the stairs.

On the top landing, light was coming from beneath the door and they caught the low murmur of voices. Cambell held the rifle across

his body, checked the other two standing behind and on either side of him, then knocked.

From inside a voice said, "Yeah?"

"Pizza."

There was a rattle of a bolt being drawn, and
the door opened against a chain lock. It was
only opened a few inches but it was wide
enough for the barrel of the Weatherby. The
face that appeared, no more than twenty years
old, took a half second to understand what it
was pressing against his forehead, then his eyes
widened with shock.

"No noise!" It was a whisper but it cut like
steel. "Slide the chain off. Do anything else and
I'll kill you through the door." In a much louder
voice, Cambell said, "You order pizza here?"

Cambell stepped back, pointed the rifle at
the door and nodded hard at the young man.
There was a moment of hesitation, then the
door partially closed and the chain scraped in its
catch. He shoved the door wide and lunged
through, sending the youth spinning back.

Four people sitting around a table snapped
their heads up.

"Nobody moves, nobody's dead." Cambell
barked the words, then gave them a second to
understand their situation. Barney had been
worried that the masks would make them look
like a joke but he needn't have. Far from appearing comical, the smiling, bearded masks gave a
macabre touch to the sight of three men dressed
in denims and boots and carrying guns. The

people at the table obeyed the order and stayed frozen.

"On the floor. *Now!*"

The young man, terrified, quickly dropped and stretched out. A blonde girl, not much older, closed her eyes, slid back her chair, and lay down very quietly. The second and third persons at the table, all hair and beards and wearing army fatigue jackets, joined her. The fourth, a black man a good ten years older than the others, stayed where he was. Cambell could see he only had one person to beat. He spoke to him slowly, his words weighted.

"Need help getting there?"

Almost lazily the black got off his chair and eased himself down onto his stomach, but he kept his face toward Cambell.

"I'm going to ask a fast question and I want a fast answer. Where's the stuff?"

With no emotion in his voice, the black said, "Now just what kind of stuff would that be?"

Cambell didn't waste time on him. He took a fast stride forward and shoved the barrel of the Weatherby against the young man's neck.

"In the garage, right?"

"Right, right." The kid couldn't talk fast enough.

"And you've got the key, haven't you?"

"No, Al's got it. I swear." He flicked his eyes toward the black man, who looked away in disgust.

Cambell slapped Dourian on the shoulder

and told him to get them. Dourian fished a hand into the man's jacket and got lucky first time.

"Frisk him," Cambell said.

Dourian had never frisked anybody in his life, but he'd been frisked himself flying out of Kennedy and he simply did what the security people did there. When he felt the hard bulge at the back of the man's belt, he flipped the jacket up and took out the small revolver that was buttoned into a hip holster. He slipped it into his own belt and stepped away. On the other side of him Barney breathed easier. There was no problem here, they had these people buffaloed. All that remained now—

The sudden honking of a horn stopped him cold. Two short bleeps. Loder. Cambell backed toward the door and positioned himself behind it. He used his head to point where he wanted them: against the walls and out of sight of the doorway.

They heard footsteps coming up the stairs, then voices; deep, maybe three or four.

Cambell brought the big rifle up to his shoulder and sighted it at the leader's head. Somebody knocked and announced himself as Marty or Murphy. Cambell opened the door an inch and let the man outside push it wide and walk through. Two of them were halfway into the room before they saw anything wrong.

"All the way in," Cambell said sharply.

There were three of them. They stopped in surprise but recovered quickly, eyes darting around, bodies tensed.

"On the heads. Right now!"

They slowly raised their hands. They were big men, hard looking, two of them black. And they weren't amateurs. They were taking in the heavy rifle and the machine guns and were busy figuring the odds. They also took in the gun tucked in Dourian's belt and knew where it had come from.

The walkover that Barney had been envisaging a moment ago had been turned around into a very tight game. And what Cambell did next showed that he felt the same. He ordered them against the wall and, without giving them a chance to move, stepped toward the man nearest him and cracked the gun barrel against his cheek. The man staggered back and almost went down.

"Move when I tell you."

Cambell's action paid off. The other two men turned and leaned into the wall, the third man groggily following suit.

Cambell tapped Dourian's arm. "Down to the garage both of you. Load up." They hesitated. It seemed crazy to take the machine guns out of the room. What kind of a bluff was one unloaded rifle?

"Listen——"

"Do it!" Cambell snapped.

They hurried from the room.

One of the men against the wall, a muscular man built like a halfback, snickered. "Hey, fuckhead. You just screwed up. You only got one gun now and that ain't gonna be enough."

"Believe me, it's plenty." Cambell saw the men shifting their weight off the wall and back onto their feet. They disguised the movement, making it look like a natural result of turning their heads to talk but they were getting ready to jump him, it was plain. He wasn't worried about the man he'd hit, he was really using the wall for support, a trickle of blood coming from the blue lump on his cheekbone. And the other man, the one called Al, was still stretched out and in no position to make a move. That left two to deal with and it was one too many. He knew, by the way they were talking, that they were both carrying guns, and he couldn't take them away because he'd have to get too close.

The big man started in again. "That rifle you got there . . ." they were trying to keep him talking . . . "that's a bolt action, man. You'll only get one of us."

"That's right. But it's a four-sixty magnum. The one I get'll be wearing his ass around his ears."

The defiant light in their eyes wavered but didn't go out, and Cambell laid it on thick. "It fires a five-hundred-grain dum-dum. They use them in Africa to turn elephants around. The elephants used to keep on coming till they came up with these, now they drop like they fell off a cliff."

As the sound of the van backing into the drive came to them, he raised the rifle and aimed it right at the big man's face. "You don't believe me, take a look at the bore."

The man stared at the outsized muzzle that stared right back at him. Then he and his partner slowly relaxed, moved their weight back onto their hands, and settled into a smoldering silence.

Dourian's voice called from outside and Cambell backed toward the door.

"Okay, I'm going down those stairs. Any heads I see up here, I'll keep for a trophy." He stepped through the door, banging it closed, leaped down the stairs, and tumbled into the van. Loder took it away fast, swerved into the street, and put his foot down. Cambell shot him a question. "What kind of car they got?"

"G.T.O."

"Hang a left."

They were almost on top of the corner when Loder braked and swung the wheel hard. Behind them one of the men had come pounding down the drive, stopped, steadied a gun in two hands, and fired twice. He would have hit them if a car parked at the corner hadn't been in the line of fire. Glass shattered as the shots slammed into it.

"Left again."

Loder swung into the street that paralleled the one the house was on. It was a half block, no more than sixty feet long, and they took another left at the top then another as they came back onto the original street, their speed cut down for the turn. Ahead of them a white G.T.O. was skewering left at the corner. They turned right at the same corner and kept on going.

"Holy Christ," Dourian said. He peeled off his mask and slumped back against the seat. "I thought you were going back for Green Stamps."

They all had their masks off now. "I thought we'd never make it," Barney said. "I never thought we'd get out of there alive."

Neither had Loder. "When those guys showed up, I didn't know what to do. What the hell happened up there?"

Barney and Dourian told him, talking over each other, Loder joining in, the pent-up tension coming out of them in a tumble of words. Cambell gave them a few minutes to get it out of their systems then asked how many rounds they'd got.

"Must be a couple of thousand," Barney answered. "They had about a dozen M Sixteens in that garage and some heavier stuff too. They were loaded for bear."

"If we hadn't had to leave so fast," Dourian said, "maybe we could have used some of it."

Cambell reached for the road map. "Maybe. We'll know shortly."

"What's that supposed to mean?"

"We're on a double date tonight."

He gave Loder some directions that took them across Mount Vernon and through a belt of woods that flanked a parkway. There was a small lake on their right where the Bronx River swelled; Barney remembered taking the kids skating there once. Loder slowed the van and the headlights picked up a rutted track, which Cambell told him to take. It led to a low building that looked like it might house maintenance equipment.

"Flash your lights," Cambell said.

From the side of the building headlights flashed back. Cambell got out and moved away in the darkness and was gone a good five minutes. When he returned, they heard an engine start, and a pickup truck moved past and stopped behind them. Cambell opened its tailgate and transfered several bundles into the back of the van. He closed the tailgate, slapped a hand against it, and the pickup drove away. For all they saw of the driver, a robot could have been behind the wheel.

"Home?" Loder asked.

"Yeah. And stay under the limit."

They bumped back onto the road and turned into the parkway entrance a hundred yards ahead. Barney looked over his shoulder at the bundles. "How did we do? Good or bad?"

"A little of both," Cambell said.

Chapter Sixteen
Day Four

It wasn't Cambell's voice that woke them in the morning but the sound of him hammering in the trees. They knew it was Cambell because they went and checked, knowing that it'd be good for fifty squat jumps each if they didn't. They had a vague idea they just might be rewarded for their vigilance by being let off the morning run and the PT, but they weren't really surprised when he put them through it. Still, breakfast was a lot brighter than it had been at any other time. Buoyed by the successful raid of the night before they felt they'd had a baptism by fire and had proved themselves, even though the fire had only been the two shots that had hit a parked car. Their new confidence showed through on the rifle range, Barney and Loder both riddling their targets. Dourian got to shoot, too. Cambell's supplier had come up with a hundred rounds for the Weatherby, which meant that if they'd met him earlier they could have gone into that house with a loaded gun. Not that it made any difference now.

Dourian hit on seven out of twelve on the rapid, and Cambell left him with a box of ammo and instructions to make it nine out of twelve. He led the other two up one of the trails through the pines, and they found out why he'd bought the plywood sheets and what all the hammering had been about. He took Barney first. He told him to walk ahead of him and fire at a target when he saw one. They started off up the trail, and a few yards farther on Cambell reached down for a rope concealed on the ground and yanked on it. A target swung out suddenly on Barney's left and he swung toward it, the machine gun chattering. They walked over to inspect it. It was a sheet of plywood with the outline of a man drawn on it. The wood was mounted on a crosspiece and hinged to a tree like a door. The board was untouched, but the tree to the right of it had four chunks gouged out. Cambell told him to bring the gun on line before he fired, to wait that fraction of a second. Then they started off again. He'd rigged up three more targets, one on the left, two on the right. Barney caught a piece of the second and hit the silhouette on the last two.

When it was Loder's turn, he had the same problem for a start, got the same advice, then improved. Cambell walked them through the course several times, Barney getting a better score going to his left, Loder doing better firing to his right—which seemed to settle something for Cambell.

They put in another hour and shot the targets to pieces, Cambell telling them they could replace them later. Right now he had another chore for them. He called Dourian over and took them up the trail to a spot where he'd marked several trees. He told them he wanted the trees cut down and cleared; they were to cut them off level with the ground, trim the branches and haul the trees away. He wanted the exact same thing done on the other side of the slope; he took them over there and showed them. The trail on that side was newer and not as distinct, but both trails roughly paralleled each other running from the road through the pines and ending where the trees thinned out on each side of the big cabin. It was a major job and even with the chain saw to cut and trim, it was getting dark as they finished. What they wound up with were two oval-shaped clearings in the forest, the one on the right about sixty yards from the cabin, the one on the left a bit closer. Why Cambell had wanted them anyway was a subject of discussion at dinner.

They were getting the hang of living in their rough quarters and even though they missed a hot shower—the best they could do was to heat some water and scrub down—they didn't give up anything in the eating department. The refrigerator was old but worked fine and kept the steaks they'd bought in good condition. They usually barbecued them on a wood fire. The butane stove was fine for potatoes and vegetables, and for dessert they ate fruit; so the meals were well balanced and hearty. They'd even gotten used to drinking milk with them.

Dourian, freshly scrubbed, pleasantly tired, and with a good dinner inside him, sipped at his Nescafe and speculated about their recent efforts. "You know," he said, "clearing trees isn't a nutty thing like some of the other stuff he's had us doing. I mean, a lot of people clear trees."

"Absolutely," Barney said. "Some of the other things, okay, a little strange. But thinning out trees, hell, it's done all the time."

Tom Loder agreed.

The raid on the house down in Woodlawn had changed their feelings toward Cambell. Before, they'd regarded him as nothing but a slave driver who was being paid to do a job and didn't bring much in the way of courtesy or consideration to it. But last night they'd seen that his toughness wasn't just verbal; as Dourian had said, the guy had *chutzpah* like mother used to make.

"We found out what the plywood was for," Loder pointed out, "and that turned out to be perfectly logical. The corrugated sheeting's probably for targets, too."

"Exactly," Dourian said. "There's probably a perfectly logical explanation for everything he's got us doing. The apple corers, the tent poles, even that hole in the roof up there."

A loud, metallic crash sounded from outside

and the three men jumped to take a look. Campbell was standing a few feet from the doorway holding a wheelbarrow. He'd just dumped a dozen thick iron pipes onto the ground.

"Dourian," he said. "Sometime tomorrow morning take these pipes and jam them into the top of the chimney."

Then he turned and pushed the wheelbarrow back toward his cabin.

Dourian shook his head at the retreating figure. Under his breath he said, "Son of a bitch. You had to go and do it, didn't you?"

Chapter Seventeen
Day Five

In the long list of complaints they could have drawn up about their stay so far, one thing that wouldn't have made it was the weather. They'd had a succession of faultless summer days with the heat holding off; so it was no surprise to wake up to another bright morning. But what was surprising was that they woke up five minutes before Cambell was due and didn't have to be kicked out of bed. Another surprise was that the aches and pains that normally accompanied the run to the fence and the calisthenics were hardly noticeable anymore. In fact, the three of them felt pretty good. The active life they'd been living, plus the high protein, alcohol-free diet, had taken a few pounds off everybody, and they were in better shape than any of them could remember.

Their mental attitude got a lift, too. Cambell finally explained everything. After breakfast he sat them down in front of his cabin, ignored the canvas-wrapped bundles that lay at his feet, and, as usual, began without any warm-up.

"When you train a boxer, you teach him a jab one day, a hook the next, a combination the next. You don't give it to him all at once, plus the fight plan. That's why I haven't told you why you've been doing all those jobs. But everything has been for one purpose only, to try to get you through a combat situation if you get into one. Naturally, if Ripoll goes for this deal you say you're going to offer him, then you just pick up and go home, no problem. But if he turns it down, your only alternative, as Rivers explains it, is to invite him up here for a chat. And if he comes, you'll have a fight on your hands. So for any of this to make sense, we're going to assume he's coming. Okay. If there was an ounce of soldier in any of you, you'd have guessed long ago that what we've been doing is setting up an ambush." He paused to let them get their minds around it.

"For an ambush to work properly, you need three things—speed, surprise, confusion. You let them win a few points, you suck them in, then you hit them hard and keep on hitting them. Normally, you'd entice the enemy into a cutoff position, but seeing as how there are three of you and twenty-five of them that won't be possible. So you'll have to do something else. You'll have to let them come damn close to overrunning your cabin. If you let them too close, you'll lose. If you don't let them close enough, you'll lose. Your only hope is to destroy them while they're trying." Again he paused. "To do that you have to be able to control where they move and how they move, and it starts with where they park their cars. That's why you repaired the fence. It's a natural stopping place, and you don't want them driving up the slope, at least not yet."

"Not yet?" Dourian was fishing for an explanation, but Cambell didn't bite.

"Rivers, you'll be in this cabin. Dourian will be in the foxhole between here and the big cabin where Loder will be."

"But if we split up——" Loder began.

"Wait. Ripoll doesn't know how many you are. He knows Rivers is here because Rivers will have told him, but he won't be expecting anybody else. So okay, he arrives in force. Rivers, you'll talk to him for starters."

"And he'll kill me for starters."

"I don't mean face-to-face. I have four walkie-talkies. You'll have one; Ripoll will have one. And Loder and Dourian will each have one so they can hear what's happening and get a jump on the action. What I'm giving you now is only my idea of how it could go. It could be a whole different ball game, but we have to work from something."

They saw the sense in that and waited to hear what he had in mind.

"He's come for your head; so after you've said hello and the amenities have been observed, he'll send in men after you. Or he may send them in right away, I don't know. But whatever, you open up on them."

"Nice. They won't be expecting a machine gun."

"Not with that," Cambell said. "With the thirty-two we took off that guy last night."

"That thing? What am I going to hit with that?"

"Nothing. The idea is to keep them coming, remember? Give them some initial success."

Barney wasn't serious, but almost. "They get me as a come-on?"

"That depends on how fast you hit that hole." He was talking about the one Barney had practiced diving into. "You start firing the thirty-two. When you run out of ammo and they rush you, you jump for the hole. That's Dourian's cue."

Dourian picked it up. "I jump up and let them have it with the Weatherby."

"Not the Weatherby," Cambell said. "With this." He stooped and unwrapped one of the canvas bundles.

Dourian whistled. "Now that's what I call a shotgun."

"It's not a shotgun. It's a grenade launcher." The weapon was simple enough; it looked like a short rifle whose barrel had been replaced by a fat piece of pipe. Cambell picked it up.

"The M Seventy-nine. It fires a forty-mil, high-explosive grenade, and it'll hit anything right on the button up to four hundred yards. But to guarantee a hit, you're firing from fifty yards, which is point-blank. That's why you need that hole, Dourian, because when a forty mil grenade goes off, you need all the protection you can get."

Barney looked unhappy. "Hell, it's going off just a few feet from me. I'm going to need a concrete bunker."

"You'll be okay as long as you stay down."

Loder raised a point. "It's going to be close. If George fires late, the Pachones will be swarming all over Barney. And if he fires too soon, Barney will go up with the cabin."

"That's right," Cambell answered. "The timing has to be perfect. So we'll have a few more rehearsals."

Understandably, Barney didn't like the part that had been picked for him, but his offer to trade places with Dourian was politely rejected. Cambell took Dourian through the loading of the weapon, showed him how to break it at the breech and insert the grenade and the cartridge that fired it. The grenade itself looked like a miniature artillery shell. Dourian asked Cambell how many he'd been able to get.

"One."

"One?"

Cambell said, "Buying arms isn't like shopping at the A&P. You ask for what you want and take what you can get. I wanted a case of inert rounds, blanks, so you'd know what it could do. All I could get was one live round."

"So it's hit or miss," Barney said.

"That's right. I don't know how I'm supposed

to train a man on a weapon without him firing it, but, Dourian, you're just going to have to do everything right the first time."

"Including not hitting me when I come through the door," Barney added.

"If it's dark," Dourian said, "that might be a problem."

"I'm counting on it being dark," Cambell told them. "If they come at all, they'll come at night. That's what our Intelligence says and we've got to go with it." He searched their faces. "Understand it, this is going to be a night combat situation."

"Does that work for us or against us?"

"It'll work for you. The Pachones will only have their car headlights. You can do better than that——I'll take you through that part later. Let's get back to where we were."

Behind Cambell, leaning against the cabin wall, was a piece of plywood. When he turned it around, they recognized a sketch of their camp. It was done simply but in some detail, with the pines chalked in on both sides of the slope, the loop road at the bottom, the cabins, the two diagonal ditches, and the two foxholes. He took a stick of chalk from his pocket and began to explain, illustrating his plan with arrows and crosses.

"All right. The cars pull up here. I'll rig lights so you can see what they're doing. Ripoll sees one man, one cabin, it looks like a pushover. When he finds out you're only armed with a Saturday Night Special, he knows it's a pushover. He sends a few of his heavies for you, and as they're coming in the front door you're going out the back and diving for your foxhole, here. Dourian puts a grenade into the cabin and it's three down, twenty-two to go. A beat later you're out of there and into the pines. Dourian, you're doing the same thing at the same time, just as we practiced. You both get on up the trail to the cabin, and while you're getting there, Loder starts firing down the middle."

Loder grinned. "It'll be a little different from the thirty-two."

"No, it won't. You're going to be firing on semiautomatic, one round at two-second intervals, and you're going to be firing at what's left of the cabin."

"I'd have thought that that was the time to hit them with everything we've got. Follow up on the surprise of the cabin."

Cambell fixed Loder with an unwavering glare. "Now get this. The last thing you want them to know is that you're sitting on a couple of machine guns. It's not the kind of thing that invites anybody to keep coming, and you've got to keep them coming. I don't care if they line up like the Rockettes, you fire short and you miss. You don't want them to think you've got Annie Oakley up here. On semiautomatic the M Sixteen sounds a lot like a deer rifle. Fine. Let them think that. You have to make them believe it's going to be a piece of cake, until they find out too late."

Barney pointed to the grenade launcher. "But

when that thing goes off and the cabin goes up, they'll know we've got a lot more than a deer rifle."

"I don't think so. At fifty yards the launcher firing and the grenade hitting will sound almost like one. They won't see any muzzle flash because Dourian will be out of their line of sight. When they hear Loder firing, they'll figure a rifle bullet hit some explosive in the cabin. Or they could think the cabin was booby-trapped and went off prematurely. But whatever, they're not going to figure a grenade launcher."

Dourian suggested that they could spot them making for the pines.

"I doubt it. You only have ten yards to cover. But even if they do, they'll only see two unarmed men. You'll leave the launcher in the foxhole." He turned back to the board and picked up where he'd left off. "Okay, so the three of you are now in the big cabin, Loder's still firing and the Pachones are behind their cars thinking about it. Again, I can only guess at how they'll react, but there are certain assumptions we can make. They'll scatter at the first shot and they'll shoot out the spotlight. That's basic. Then they'll move on the cabin. From what Rivers tells me, these people are basically a collection of hit men who've been trained to kill but not necessarily to fight, which is to your advantage. And Ripoll's not likely to know much about tactics, but he'll use his common sense. I think it's ten to one he'll split them up and send them at the cabin in a pincer movement."

"That sounds exactly like a military tactic to me," Barney said.

"Well, sure it is, but it's a natural thing to do. You don't have to know that Hannibal beat the Romans with it or that Hindenburg used it to destroy two Russian armies. The Double Flank Envelopment is a fundamental maneuver even if you just call it sneaking up on two sides."

"Would they be better to come at us from one side?"

"Nope. They'll be doing the right thing. It's a smart move when you have superior numbers."

"But there must be examples of the underdog coming out on top."

"Sure. Darius, Wellington, Kliest, and Guderian, they all did the trick. But then they were generals. I'm only a sergeant." That stopped the questions for a while and Cambell moved chalk over his sketch.

"Ripoll isn't going to send all his men against one rifle, but any man who has twenty-five bodyguards goes in for overkill; so let's say he sends five up the right side, five up the left, and breaks out the rifles to give them diversionary fire. Dourian, this is where you come in. They have to bring their handguns close to count on doing any real damage, but a good man with a rifle can lay back there behind those cars and pick you off. You have to knock them out."

"I can knock out the man maybe but not the

weapon. Somebody else will just pick those rifles up."

"Yes, but they won't be riflemen; so they won't be as effective. You, on the other hand, have to be very effective. You'll be firing from the roof of the cabin; so besides the heavy rifle you'll also have the advantage of elevation. The chimney will be your cover. It's good and wide and those flagstones are pretty solid."

Dourian tapped his forehead. "That's why the hole in the roof. And those iron pipes are in the chimney to shore it up."

Cambell nodded. "That's also why you cut up the iron sheeting. We'll nail it to the inside of the cabin wall and stack those boxes of earth behind it. The cabin's only pine and that won't stop anything. The sheeting will take the sting out of a slug and those boxes should trap it. For a start, anyway. I wouldn't want to guarantee them holding up under sustained rifle fire. The Pachones have Remington seven forty-twos that are gas operated and will fire four rounds as fast as a man can pull the trigger. If they've got them chambered for the three-O-eight Winchester slug, you're going to have your hair full of dirt."

He gave them a moment to digest that piece of information, then listened as Barney got back to his original point.

"So now they hear another rifle, and a big one. How are they going to react to that? The ones coming up the trails."

"They're not under fire; so it shouldn't bother

them. It's one more rifle to take care of, big deal. And they won't know any different till they get to here." Cambell chalked a cross on the two clearings in the trails. "That's when they'll run into a little surprise. If it works like it should, it'll take out three or four of them on each side."

All three of them looked down at the other bundle on the ground, but if that was the surprise Cambell was talking about, he was saving it till later.

Dourian said, "The game will change then. They'll know for sure that things ain't what they seem."

"Correct. But they'll still figure they've got you pinned down in that cabin, and they'll be right. But what they won't realize is that you've purposely put yourselves in that position so as to force them to fight on your terms."

Loder smiled. "That's not bad. Which general thought of that?"

"He wasn't a general, he was a corporal." Cambell turned back to his sketch. "Now things begin to get tough for them. They'll start running into some trip wires I'm going to rig around here where the pines thin out. They'll be connected to hi-beam flashlights I'll wire overhead. They'll shoot them out fast enough, but they'll have to do it while they're running for cover. That's when Rivers and Loder will go to Automatic and open up. Rivers, you'll take the left side, Loder the right. And you'll stick to those sides. I don't care if it's World War Three on the left and nothing on the right, you look only after your own sector. Okay." Cambell drew an arrow that started at the fence and continued up the middle toward the cabin. "When Ripoll hears machine guns, he'll bring his armor into action."

He answered the question before anybody asked it.

"I'm talking about their cars. Bombproof and bulletproof, with two-inch armor plate. They probably have steel shields that come down over the windows, too; so they're really a fortress on wheels. With a driver and a man with a rifle inside they could bull through that fence, come up the middle, park on your doorstep, and blow your stuff away. That's why you dug those two ditches here. We'll hammer the tent poles in all the way along them and cap them with the apple corer blades. They won't spot them till they're right on top of them, and they won't want to take their tires out; so they'll swing and go for the opening we've left. And that'll give you a broadside shot."

They were happy to finally have the strange purchases explained, and Cambell's improvisation was clever. But there was a point that bothered them all, especially Dourian.

"It's going to have to be some shot. I don't see stopping them unless I hit the tires."

"Forget the tires." Cambell unwrapped the other bundle on the ground. "It doesn't matter where you hit them with this." The thing he unwrapped looked like a short mailing tube with a shoulder piece and a handgrip attached.

Loder frowned at it. "That will stop an armored Cadillac?"

"It'll stop a tank. This is a Law, the baby of the Dragon Weapons System. What it really is, is a portable missile launcher. It fires a finned rocket with a self-contained warhead and propulsion system. It sounds fancy, but it's simple enough to use." He picked up the instrument and demonstrated. "To cock it you pull it out of its telescope, which pops the sights up as you can see. You connect these two terminals here, hold it into your shoulder, and press down on the plunger. Think you can do all that, Dourian?"

"Another one for me? I'm going to need a native bearer."

"You get the grenade launcher and this antitank because they're both fired like rifles. And you're the rifleman of this outfit."

Dourian asked how the weapon was loaded.

"It comes that way, preloaded. There's a sixty-six-mil Heat round in here that's powerful enough to blast through a foot of armor plating; so it shouldn't have any problem knocking over a car."

"What if they send two cars, or three? How do I reload?"

"You don't. This is a disposable weapon; you use it and dump it. It's strictly a one-shot item."

"So we need a whole new launcher?"

"Right."

Barney supplied the clincher. "But we don't have one. . . ."

"Right again," Cambell said. He didn't have to repeat the facts of life regarding the purchase of military weapons; they understood you couldn't pick and choose. Nevertheless, the fact was plain to see: They had one missile to handle four cars and that wasn't going to be enough.

Loder, trying to look on the bright side, said, "Well, if they send one car for a start, and George knocks it out, maybe they'll think twice about sending another."

Cambell agreed. "That's what I'm counting on. They won't know you only have one A.T."

Barney snapped his fingers; he thought he'd seen a way out. "Why don't we save the grenade launcher for the cars. Blow the cabin up with something else."

It was Cambell's turn to pose a question, which he did with a tired patience. "Like what, for instance?"

"I don't know. Couldn't we get some dynamite from somewhere?"

"Sure," Cambell answered. "Run down to the store and buy two sticks."

Barney didn't offer any further suggestions and Cambell wasn't listening anyway; he was busy talking again.

"Regardless what happens to the cars, you've still got your hands full. You've got men on both sides of you, and they're close and they're hungry. It'll be up to Rivers and Loder to handle them because you're going to have to get a lot of bullets out there fast. I'll show you how to tape three magazines together that will give you ninety rounds apiece, which should be plenty if you watch your rate of fire." He tapped the board with the chalk and stood aside. "So there it is. I'm not saying it's going to happen that way, I'm saying that it could. But you're going to have to be ready for whatever does happen. It's not a rosy picture, I grant you. There are still too many of them and not enough of you. But you'll have surprise on your side for one thing and you'll be taking the initiative for another, and if it makes you feel any better, the tactic you're going to be using has worked pretty well before."

"Does it have a name?" Loder asked. "The tactic?"

"Attack from a Defensive Position. It worked for Caesar; it worked for Rommel. It turned the trick at Bannockburn, Crecy, Poitiers, Agincourt." Cambell stopped and swept his eyes over the grass slope and the pines and the big cabin standing under the cliff. "Whether it will turn the trick at Little Bear Lake is something I'm not going to promise."

He rolled up the two weapons and took them inside, leaving them contemplating the chalked arrows and crosses. They looked like three members of a hopelessly overmatched football team studying a brave game plan. While they'd been impressed by the depth of Cambell's thinking and surprised by his knowledge of historical

213

warfare, the plan raised as many questions as it answered. If it didn't go the way he predicted—if Ripoll threw them a curve—how were they to react? And with Cambell gone, who was going to tell them what to do? It was abundantly clear that Cambell's description of the picture as less than rosy was quite an understatement. The picture was decidedly bleak.

He saved them from further speculation when he came out carrying a small box, which they hadn't seen before. He led them down the slope and started talking again.

"When you go into night combat, you need something better than your own eyes. I can give you a ground flare and a flare pistol, and I can rig lights like I told you, but I can't light the place like Shea Stadium. What you really need is a night scope, but they cost the army seven thousand bucks new; so they don't leave them lying around."

Barney repeated the figure. "They must really be something."

"They're a small miracle. They take the ambient light in the sky, moonlight, starlight, cloud reflection, and magnify it millions of times. If you had a couple of those to use against the Pachones, you'd have an early night."

Barney glanced at the box. "Is that something like it?"

"It's a poor substitute."

Cambell stopped about thirty yards short of the fence, opened the box, and took out a plastic cylinder about the size and shape of a can of beans. From the bottom of the device he extracted three long spikes that he pushed into the ground; then he pulled out a tiny aerial that was telescoped into the top.

"A geophone," he said. "A vibration sensor. It picks up ground vibrations and relays them back to a receiver console you'll have in your cabin. We'll leave this one here in case they try to come up the middle, and we'll put one half a mile up the road."

Loder got it right away. "An early warning system for their cars. Cute."

Cambell flicked a switch on the sensor. "As a watchdog it's fine. But for more sophisticated work it has its drawbacks, the main one being it takes a while to learn to decipher its signals. It'll pick up anything that moves at a hundred yards, a car, a man, an animal, a falling branch. But it can't tell you what it is, and it can't tell you how close it is until you learn to read the console."

They walked back to the little cabin where Cambell produced another of his canvas-wrapped bundles. This one contained a foot-square metal box. He extended the tripod that was built into it and set it down on the grass. On the face of the box were four dials, one beneath the other, on the right-hand side. Opposite each one, in horizontal line, was a small glass button and a rocker switch. On top of the box a circular aerial projected; he raised it several inches. As he did that he spoke to Loder.

"You're used to hardware; so you're the best

man for this job. But you're going to have to learn fast to be any good at it."

He told Barney and Dourian to walk down toward the sensor he'd stuck into the ground. Then he flicked a switch on the console and it hummed into life. A needle on a dial lifted fractionally and quivered. When the two men were almost on top of the sensor, the needle leaped up the face of the gauge and the glass button next to it glowed red. At the same time a bleeper sounded softly at half-second intervals.

"Two visual signals, one audio signal," Loder said. "Seems simple enough."

"It gets harder."

Cambell called to Barney and Dourian to back off and run on the spot. This time the console appeared to react the same as it had before.

"I see what you mean," Loder said. "There's very little definition between signals."

Cambell nodded. "That's the hangup with this equipment, and there's no quick fix. It takes time to train a man to tell the difference, and time's what we're short of around here. So we'd better start now."

They spent the rest of the morning at it and a good part of the afternoon, too. Then Cambell switched him to the range, showing Barney and him how to use their machine guns with three magazines taped together. He had them walk each other through the course, then worked with Dourian from his new position up on the roof. Cambell had found an old ladder, which he'd cut down and fixed into position inside. It made getting up on the roof a lot easier. He showed him how to snuggle himself in behind the chimney and how to adjust his shooting for the downhill line.

They ate dinner and, when it was good and dark, he got them onto night firing, spotting the targets at quick, irregular intervals with a high power flashlight. Then he put Loder back onto the console and drilled him in reading the dials by the glow of the instrument lights. Loder understood the machine, but it was hard to pick up fast and it gave him a lot of trouble.

It was close to ten before Cambell finally called it a day. Nobody gave him an argument; they were bushed. They killed the lights and crawled into bed and lay there thinking over what Cambell had told them that day.

"Barney," Dourian said, "when are you going to call Ripoll?"

"Day after tomorrow," Barney answered. Then he added, as wrong as ever, "Madison won't have heard from Switzerland yet."

The talk was replaced by yawns and the scrunch of bedsprings, and not long after, they drifted off. Over in the corner of the room the detector console sat on its tripod, its needles and buttons dead. But hours later, the birds not yet awake, the night silent, the stars high in their inky blackness, one of the buttons began to glow.

As the glow brightened and blossomed into a fiery red, the needle in the gauge next to it quivered and rose and flickered violently back

217

and forth, like a dumb man waving a frantic arm in the dark.

With no sound the figure came toward the cabin. If there'd been a moon breaking quickly through a patch of cloud, it might have glinted for a brief moment on what the man held in his hand. The bottom step creaked under his weight and he froze and stayed that way for a minute, then continued up the steps. He closed a hand over the door latch and with painful care pressed it open. He slipped through the door, easing it closed behind him. From his belt he took a small flashlight and hooded it with his fingers. It threw a feeble light on the three figures, shapeless bundles under rumpled sheets. The man crept closer, the light resting for a quick moment on each of their faces. Then the man moved toward Barney, stretched out on his back, one arm dangling. He stood over the sleeping figure and slowly brought his hand up, moved the thing in his hand toward Barney's head and pressed it against his neck.

"Huh?" Barney's eyes flickered, the rest of him still asleep. The pressure increased and his eyes opened wider, sudden comprehension shocking him wide awake. He choked out a cry and threw an arm up but hit only air. Then the lights clicked on and Barney, bolt upright, fright widening in his eyes, sagged back onto the mattress.

"Oh, Jesus," he said. "Oh, my God. You just took ten years off my life."

Cambell lowered the automatic. "If I'd been you-know-who I'd have taken forty years off it."

Loder and Dourian, coming slowly awake, peered around them.

"What's up?" Loder mumbled.

Cambell strode over to the detector box. "Look at this thing. Useless. I spend all day taking you through it and what happens? You leave the audio off. Did you think you were going to read the needle through your eyelids?"

Barney, still recovering, said, "Why sneak up on me? I'm not in charge of that gizmo."

"You're in charge of this group. It's up to you to see that Loder has the detector working properly and that Dourian doesn't turn the hardware into a clothes rack."

One of Dourian's socks had slipped off a chair and fallen over the grenade launcher. Cambell whipped it off and threw it up at Dourian.

"Any day now you could have a couple of dozen killers on your doorstep. It's a definite possibility but you don't believe it. You go on thinking that and you could end up very surprised and very dead. I'm not going to tell you that again."

He walked out of the cabin, leaving them looking at each other.

Dourian said, "Barney, enough is enough. It's four thirty in the morning and a man has just come in and complained about my socks. I've had it."

"I'm with you, George," Loder said. With a sigh he got out of bed and flicked a switch on the detector. "I'll tell you, I'm not coming back here next year."

Barney struggled to a sitting position. "Look, I know how you feel. If you want a real thrill, try waking up to a gun at your head. But it's only two more days. Forty-eight hours. That's all we have to get through."

"It'd better be," Dourian said, "because I'm up to here with this cold-water cabin and its cold-water shaves and immortal Sergeant York jawing at me day and night. Forty-eight hours and I'm out of here. And that's a promise."

Forty-eight hours. Twenty-four Colts, four Remingtons, a shotgun, and four armored Cadillacs. And Dourian was complaining about cold water.

Chapter Eighteen
Day Six

They started on the cabin after breakfast. They worked quickly and without complaint, resolved to get through the two days as painlessly as they could. With Cambell directing them, they removed all the glass from the windows, carried in the corrugated sheets, and nailed them up securely. They covered the entire front wall of the main room, leaving only two narrow apertures at the windows to serve as gun ports. It took away their front door, leaving the side door in the bedroom as the only exit. They moved in the earth-filled boxes and stacked them against the sheeting, the ends with the griddle plates facing into the cabin. They packed them tightly together from floor to shoulder height.

Then they went outside and started on the ditches. They took all the tent poles Cambell had bought and hammered them in at three-foot intervals, angling them at thirty degrees. They pinched an apple corer blade onto the top of each one, and when they had finished they walked off and took a look. Two rows of very formidable looking stakes pointed at them, the sharp metal tips glinting in the sunlight. Except for the short gap in the center, they blocked the entire approach to the cabin.

Cambell had Loder dig a small hole right where they were standing and sent the other two to his cabin. They came back carrying a large wheel of electrical wire and a canvas bag. When the hole was about a foot and a half deep, Cambell took what looked like a long white candle from the bag and planted it.

"Air Force flare," he explained. "Turns night into day for about ninety seconds."

He unrolled a few feet of wire from the wheel, taped an electric detonator to the top of the flare and connected it up. He drove the wire into the ground with an earth pin, and Barney and Dourian backed off with the wheel, paying out wire over the ditch and all the way to the cabin. Cambell and Loder followed, hammering in pins every thirty feet. Cambell cut the wire at the cabin and took it up through a loose floorboard. Inside, he attached the end to two flashlight batteries, rigged up a switch, and taped the apparatus to the detector console. That done, he led them outside again and down the trail through the pines on the right-hand side to the clearing they'd made.

He said, "I told you that the Pachones would

run into a little surprise." He set down the canvas bag. "This is it." He pulled out a small green box, plastic on its concave front, steel on its straight back. It was the size and shape of a portable cassette player and it looked about as dangerous.

"I'll bite," Dourian said. "What is it?"

"It's a Claymore mine. Antipersonnel."

"Oh," Dourian said, unimpressed. "Which means you want another hole dug."

"You don't bury a Claymore." Cambell unfolded the four sharp prongs that were hinged into the underside and showed them what you did do with it. He slammed it into a tree driving the spikes deep into the trunk, pushing his weight against it till it was set in solid. He'd chosen a tree that was on the far side of the clearing for anybody coming up the trail toward the cabin. He positioned the mine about waist high, got down behind it, peeped through the sight on the side and angled it to face directly into the open space.

"It's really just a shotgun," he told them, "only on a lot bigger scale. There's three pounds of compressed high explosive in the back here, and when that's detonated it blows pellets out the front. They're like steel marbles, and they get blasted out so hard and fast any one of them's lethal at thirty yards."

Loder asked him how many it fired.

"Seven hundred."

All three men winced.

"It's choked like a shotgun, too," Cambell

said. "The shot hits over an area roughly eight feet high by twelve wide."

"Antipersonnel," Barney said. "Good name."

Cambell finished with the mine, crossed the clearing, and stopped ten yards down the trail. He took a sensor from his bag and planted it at the base of a tree.

"The mines are fired electronically, which means you, Loder. You'll get a reading on the detector when the Pachones get close. If you misread the signals, you may only get one man, and that's no good. You've got to take them out in clumps."

They followed him out of the trees and across the slope to the clearing on the other side, where he rigged another mine and planted its sensor. Then he took Loder back to the cabin, taped an electronic switch to the console and showed him how it worked. With Barney and Dourian running up and down the trails, he drilled Loder in reading the signals from the new sensors, but Loder was still learning very slowly.

They spent the rest of the morning at it and half of the afternoon, before getting back to the guns again. When they knocked off for dinner, Barney told Cambell that he had to go into town to call his family at Diamond Point and left Dourian behind to drill Loder. They gave him messages to pass on, and half an hour later he was doing just that from the phone booth in Lake George.

He told Peggy Loder the same thing he told his wife, that the free-lance project he and Tom were working on was keeping them in town for another weekend. When he spoke to Amanda, she couldn't say much with the others in the room, but he told her that everything was fine and that he was sure George would be coming for her in a few days' time. He talked with his daughter, hearing about a rattler that had turned out to be a lizard, gave his son some advice on the right bait for bass, then hung up feeling lousy. And mad. He began to feel that if he had to spend one more hour around Cambell and his hardware, he'd go through the roof.

On the spur of the moment he picked up the phone, got a better idea, hung it up, went out and got into the van. He went half a mile to the highway, turned south, and arrived at Saratoga Springs thirty minutes later. He coasted through the town to the old part, past the stately frame houses and the beautiful parks with their landscaped gardens. It seemed macabre to have come to such an elegant spot to talk to a murderer, but it was safer this way if Ripoll traced his call.

He made the call from a hotel. He got the number of the Hotel Maria and the operator dialed it for him.

A man's voice came on, a slow, bored voice. "Yes?"

"I want to speak to Luis Ripoll."

"Ripoll. Nope. Nobody by that name registered here."

"Yeah, well, while you're checking, tell him that Steven MacDonald's on the line." He figured that the fastest way of finding out if Ripoll had heard was to see if the name meant anything to him. If not he'd just have to keep calling till it did. He was wondering whether he shouldn't try to talk to him anyway, tell him that he'd lost his money, and get him to get Madison to call Switzerland and verify it. But it was an idea he didn't need.

"Mr. MacDonald?"

Just two words, five syllables, yet they were spoken with such calm assurance that there was no doubt whose voice it was. Barney was stopped by the thought that he was finally talking to the man who'd thrown his life into a turmoil the last two weeks, the man he knew was responsible for that hideous scene in that tenement bedroom. Along with this came the realization that Ripoll knew about the money.

"Ripoll?"

"You have something that belongs to me, I believe."

The accent was there, and the way he pronounced his words was unmistakably Spanish, the m's turning into n's. He used a formal style of English, but the words came easily with no hesitation.

"That's right."

"You are calling to gloat?"

"I'm calling to explain. It was a mistake, Ripoll. I thought I could make a few bucks dipping into Madison's account. It got out of hand."

"Yes. I thought it was perhaps something like that."

The man was so cool. He could have been talking about a twenty-five-dollar check that was late.

"I'll make a deal with you, Ripoll."

"A deal?" It was very effective the way he said it, as if he'd heard of the word but had never had anything to do with such a thing.

"I'll give you your money back in return for my safety."

"Agreed."

"I'm going to need more than your word, Ripoll."

"If you think I'm going to put it in writing——"

"I'm the one who's put it in writing. I'm offering you your money back in annual payments, six and a half million a year. I've left a letter with a lawyer that if anything happens to me, the balance of the money will disappear. And I've primed the bank to expect such a letter so there'll be no delay. The money will just vanish."

There was a heavy pause, and when Ripoll spoke again his voice was like an iceberg, just the tip of his anger showing.

"That is very clever of you, Señor. And very cruel."

"Cruel? What's cruel about it? Six and a half million a year tax free isn't exactly going to leave you in the poorhouse."

"What do you know about money, a cheap crook who got lucky. You're taking away my *capital!*"

The words stung Barney. He yelled into the phone.

"It's not yours, Ripoll. You stole it. But if you want it back, it'll be on my terms. So what's it going to be? Make up your mind."

He realized too late he'd been too forceful; he'd practically invited the man to turn him down. He fully expected Ripoll to tell him to keep the money and see how much good it was at protecting him, but instead the answer was a protracted silence. Then Ripoll spoke very quietly.

"You give me very little choice. Call me here at this time tomorrow and I will let you know my decision."

Ripoll hung up quickly, Barney slowly. He let himself out of the booth into the coolness of the air-conditioned lobby. When he put a hand to his forehead, it came away wet. He took a few deep breaths, settling himself down, crossed to the desk, paid for the call, and went into the hotel bar. He had a fast drink and waited for the hammering to recede in his chest, thinking how close he'd come to blowing it. He refused the bartender's offer of another drink, sat there a few minutes more, then went out to the van and drove back to the camp.

He found Dourian and Loder wondering what had taken him so long.

"I called Ripoll. He knows about the money."

He gave them a verbatim rundown on the phone call. "I'm sorry I got mad. I should have played it cooler."

"Maybe," Dourian said. "But you got results.

228

The guy knows we've got him by the short hairs. He as much admitted it. So we're home and dry."

Tom Loder thought so, too. "If he told you he had no choice then that's tantamount to accepting the deal. He's only holding you off a day to see if he can spot a loophole."

"You think he'll find one?"

"I don't see how. The thing's airtight. He just needs a little time to get used to the idea."

Cambell came in and Barney told him what he'd told the others. Cambell heard him through, then got around to the reason he was there. "Okay. Grab your weapons. We're going to have a dress rehearsal."

Dourian looked at Cambell, looked at Barney and Loder, then back at Cambell again. "You're kidding," he said. "Tonight?"

"Why, is it your bowling night?"

"Aw, come on, Cambell. We're through playing soldiers. You heard Barney, Ripoll's going to buy it. It's just sticking in his craw, that's all. When Barney calls tomorrow that'll be it, so why, for crissakes, do we have to go out and bump around in the dark now?"

"Because that phone call didn't change anything. You're still waiting on the man to give you an answer just as you were the first day you got here."

"What is this with you? All along you've been acting like you know for sure he's going to turn us down. It's like you're hoping for a fight."

In comparison to Dourian's loud voice and waving arms, Cambell was a block of wood when he replied.

"Now get this. I don't give a shit if there's a fight or not. But when I get paid to do a job I do it, and I'm being paid to train you people for seven days. Not six, seven. If you want to call it quits now, say so. Because, mister, if you end up in the dirt with a bullet in your gut, I don't want you cussing me out for shortchanging you."

Barney halted the argument. He reached for his gun, Loder following his example. "He's right, George. Come on, it's only one more day."

Dourian, seeing he was not going to get any support, raised his arms and let them fall against his sides. He settled for a grunt that said they were all crazy.

Cambell told them what he wanted. "We're going to have a run-through. Simulated combat. So far you've learned to do everything in bits and pieces. I want to see if you can put it all together. We'll use live ammo where we've got it to spare. You can't fire the grenade launcher or the A.T. or detonate the mines; so you're going to have to tell me how to do it instead of showing me. I'll be giving you directions and I want to hear how you react, loud and clear. Dourian, use the Weatherby from the hole as a substitute for the launcher."

That halted Barney. "You mean for real? He's going to fire that thing over my head?"

"If you do it right. Otherwise it'll be into your

head." He pointed a finger at Loder. "Where's your position?"

"Right cabin window."

"What are you firing? What, how, when, where?"

"Submachine gun, semiauto, two-second intervals, firing at the cabin."

"After Rivers is clear, remember. Dourian, what are you doing?"

"Weatherby from the hole into the cabin after Barney's signal. Then I get back here and up onto the roof."

"Rivers?"

"In the cabin with the thirty-two. I signal George and hit the hole. Then I make it to the pines and back here, stand by with the machine gun."

"Okay. But only one round from that revolver. Don't forget."

When Cambell had come into the room, he'd been carrying the small canvas bag they'd seen before. Now he opened it and produced a heavy, closed-flap holster on a gun belt. He told Barney to buckle it on and explained why. "If you empty that thirty-two at the Pachones, it'll leave you in the hole without a weapon. If something goes wrong, you're going to need one." He put out a hand. "Let's have it."

Barney pulled the gun from the holster and passed it over.

Cambell took him through it quickly. "A Colt forty-five automatic. You take the safety off, insert the magazine till you hear it lock, grasp

231

the slide, pull it all the way back, release it, aim, and fire." He stretched an arm out at the wall and squeezed the trigger. The hammer clicked loudly. "I'll load the mag for you later." He gave the pistol back and spoke to them all. "Now get out of here and wait for my cue. And when you go into it, I want to see it and hear it like it was for real."

Barney stuck the flashlight and the little revolver into the gun belt and followed Dourian out of the room. They trotted together down the slope, through the break between the two ditches. There was no moon and it was dark outside, but they knew the place now like the back of their hands.

"George," Barney said. He nodded at the Weatherby Dourian was carrying. "You wouldn't try to bag a buddy, would you?"

"Some buddy," Dourian grumbled.

He dropped off into his foxhole and, as Barney continued to the little cabin, slipped a clip into the Weatherby and pumped a round into the chamber. When Cambell came by, he said, "Dourian, do you owe Rivers any money?"

"Me? No."

"Then you'll have no excuse if you hit him."

He walked down to the little cabin where he joined Barney. There'd been a couple of changes made since Barney had last seen it; Cambell had nailed some sheets of corrugated iron under the window and stacked half a dozen boxes behind it. Taped to one of them was a battery switch, the wire from it disappearing into the floorboards. There was also a walkie-talkie on the floor. Cambell showed Barney how it worked and told him that the switch was for the overhead light he'd rigged up by the fence. He crossed into the tiny bedroom and came back with a box of ammunition. He asked Barney for the forty-five, ejected the magazine, and began to load it.

"You've got the toughest job. You've got to shoot at them but not hit them, and try to stay alive while they're shooting back. You'll have to get out here fast but not so fast that you shortchange Dourian on the flashlight. He's got to know when to fire." He glanced at the thirty-two in Barney's belt. "How do you use it?"

"Move the safety off and pull the trigger."

He held out the magazine. "Let's see you load the forty-five."

Barney took it, pulled out the heavy pistol, and showed him. "Insert the mag, push it in till it locks, safety off, aim, and fire."

"Aim and fire, huh?" Cambell reached for the gun and at the same time took hold of Barney's wrist. He pressed the muzzle into Barney's palm and, while Barney's expression changed from puzzlement to wild, unbelieving alarm, he thumbed back the hammer and pulled the trigger.

There was a loud click as the hammer thumped against the firing-pin stop. Barney let out a sound like "Uhhnn" and went limp.

"Know why you've still got a hand?" Cambell asked.

Barney, in shock, looked back at him.

"Because this is an automatic not a revolver. You have to cock it first time by pulling the slide back like I showed you."

"Hell of a way of demonstrating it."

"You should have remembered. Things like that'll get you killed. He handed the gun back. "Douse the lights here and hit that switch. Give me a minute to get alongside Dourian and, when I call you, start."

When he stepped out of the door, Barney killed the lights and pressed the battery switch on the box. Immediately a light sprang on in a big pine back of the fence slanting down on the loop of the road. Barney looked into the dark, trying to imagine four cars parked there, the Pachones crouching behind them, but the picture wouldn't form. He pulled the thirty-two from his belt, got the flashlight into his hand and waited, nervous. When the shout sounded from up the slope, it startled him into action.

"Rivers. *Go!*"

He thumped the switch killing the light over the road, thrust the revolver through the window, thumbed the safety, and jerked the trigger. The gun cracked loudly. He dropped it onto the floor, turned, and ran for the door. As he leaped through, he snapped the flashlight on and dived for the hole. He heard the crack of the bullet overhead a fraction before he heard the report and the sound of the slug gouging through the cabin's front wall. He scrambled up and out and ran for the trees as Loder started firing. He swung onto the trail and trotted down it, easily following its familiar twists and turns. Ahead of him, he could hear Dourian and Cambell running. He came to the clearing, suddenly very aware of the small dark shape stuck into the tree on the other side. For a brief instant, he pictured the detector in the cabin reading his approach and Tom Loder, nervous, keyed up, reacting instinctively. He bent his head, dashed past the pine, and the trees closed around him again.

He made the cabin and ran through the side door, crossed the kitchen and entered the main room. From the far window, Loder was firing, the report muffling Cambell's voice. Cambell was up on the roof with Dourian snapping out words.

"Muzzle flash, right side."

The Weatherby sounded like a bolt of thunder.

"Loder, what are you doing?"

"Holding fire."

"Rivers, where are you?"

"Left side window."

"Muzzle flash, left and center."

The big rifle fired twice.

"What are you loading?"

"Jacketeds," Dourian said.

"Loder, watch that console. Muzzle flash, right."

The rifle roared.

"Right and center."

Dourian fired twice, the bolt slamming back and forth, the ejected shells bouncing off the roof.

"Loder, second dial reading, what do you do?"

"Watch it. Wait for——"

"Third dial reading. Very strong."

"Change frequency, fire now!"

"Flash left. Left again."

The Weatherby banged in quick succession.

"Loder, second dial, red light screaming."

"Original frequency, fire!"

"Trip wires, Rivers."

Cambell's flashlight stabbed a tree on the left, and Barney chopped a burst at it. The flashlight winked off and reappeared on the right, but Loder was ready. His machine gun chattered and the light went out.

"Car up the middle, Loder."

"Battery switch. Flare."

"Coming right at us. Dourian, what do you do?"

"Antitank. Fire!"

"Trip wires, right." A machine gun exploded. "Bottom dial. Loder, what's it mean?"

"Men up the middle."

"Rivers, what do you do?"

"Flare pistol. Fire!"

"Dourian, what are you using?"

"Dumdums."

The flashlight hit on both sides and center, and the three guns hacked at the night and kept it up as the flashlight popped on and off, the machine guns melding together in a continuous barrage, the Weatherby crashing through the wall of noise.

The flashlight went out and the guns stopped, the echo caroming off the cliff behind them, billowing away as if enormous wooden barrels were being rolled down the slope.

Cambell descended the ladder, Dourian behind him, and flicked on the light. The floor was littered with cartridge shells and the air was acrid and smoky. Everybody moved through the kitchen and out through the bedroom door into the fresh air.

Dourian, in spite of his earlier reluctance, had enjoyed the exercise. "How about that for cowboys and Indians?"

"We sure got some lead out there, didn't we?" Loder said.

Barney was smiling, too. "If it had been for real, boy, would they be surprised."

"And, boy, would you be dead." Cambell let them down with a thud.

Barney didn't understand. "But we did everything you told us. George hit the cabin; I heard it. And Tom was watching the console like a hawk."

Dourian said, "Sure, and I could see the machine guns carving hunks out of those trees."

They waited for the explanation, feeling as if a big victory had been snatched away from them on a last-minute technicality. But it was more than that. Cambell set them straight.

"Two things. When I called that car coming at us up the middle, your exact words, Dourian, were 'Antitank. Fire.' You forgot about the ditches, didn't you?"

Dourian looked pained. "Goddamn it," he said.

"You were supposed to wait till it turned for the gap. You took a frontal shot and we'll score that a miss. So you let a car through. That's point one. Point two was your mistake, Loder, and it was worse than Dourian's. Your reaction to the third dial reading was 'Change frequency, fire now.' The third dial monitors the sensor on the right. You change frequency to fire the Claymore on the left. You exploded the wrong mine at the wrong time."

"Hell, I got flustered."

"Flustered," Cambell said. "Nobody was firing at you. There was nothing out there except trees." He looked around at the hangdog faces. "And you guys didn't think you needed an extra day." He shook his head. "You need an extra month."

Chapter Nineteen
Day Seven

Cambell didn't come for them the next morning and there was no run and no calisthenics. It was almost as if he were ashamed of their performance of the night before and didn't want to have anything to do with them. They caught glimpses of him in the pines, rigging trip wires; so he was still going through with his part of the bargain, but after their poor showing, and the fact they'd be calling Ripoll that evening, it seemed like wasted effort.

The three of them ate a quiet breakfast, then took a stroll around the camp to see what damage their guns had done. The Weatherby had chunked a fat hole out of the little cabin and there were smaller holes in both walls where Loder's shots had gone through. The big rifle had also ripped holes in some of the trees back of the fence, and up near the cabin where the pines thinned out, the trees were peppered from the machine guns. But it was still only something they'd seen before, firing at targets, and it didn't make them feel any better. The fact was, they'd gone the course and flunked out; and even though none of them had liked what they'd been doing, or believed in it much, it still would have been nice to have graduated.

They moped around for the rest of the day doing little jobs to kill the time, Barney and Loder taping new magazines together, Dourian dividing his bullet clips, all of them cleaning their weapons. They took another look at both cabins, trying to assess what they could repair and what they'd just have to reimburse the realtor for. They were relieved when Cambell called a weapons inspection—it gave them something to do—but whether their guns were sparkling clean or whether Cambell just didn't care anymore, he handed them back without comment and left them alone again.

The unfamiliar inactivity was making them nervous and jumpy, and it seemed to take forever for evening to come on. They had a final discussion on how to handle Ripoll if he tried to hedge or change the terms of the deal, then Barney drove off. He went only as far as Glen Falls this time, just ten miles south of Lake George. When he called the hotel and asked for Ripoll, he had to wait a minute to be transferred. In that minute he had an instant attack of nerves. This was the crunch, the moment he'd been thinking and worrying about for so long. Incredibly, now that it had arrived, it seemed to have sneaked up on him. When the phone was picked up, his stomach fluttered and he swallowed quickly.

"Luis Ripoll, please. My name's MacDonald."

"Steven MacDonald?"

"That's right."

"Ah, yes, Mr. MacDonald." It was the desk clerk speaking. "Mr. Ripoll told me you'd be calling. He left a message for you."

"He isn't there?"

"Not at the moment, no. But he told me to tell you that he accepts your offer."

"He accepts?"

"That's the message, sir. Mr. Ripoll accepts your offer."

"Thank *you*." Barney hung up, stepped out of the booth and let go the breath he'd had bottled up for a week. He felt as if he'd been crawling through a long, dark hole and had at last emerged into brilliant sunshine. He felt a lot of things, all of them part of an immense, overwhelming relief. His first thought was to call his wife and tell her the whole incredible story; hell, he could drive up there, it was only thirty minutes away. But out on the sidewalk he changed his mind; this was one thing he could never tell anybody.

With the first real smile on his face for days, he went into a liquor store and bought a bottle of gin, some tonics, a bag of ice and some newspapers, now that they were going to be rejoining the world, then drove back to Little Bear Lake.

Dourian and Loder's reaction was the same as Barney's had been: a huge, sighing relief that collapsed them both into chairs. Then the relief turned into spontaneous good humor, which was helped along by the drinks Barney made. They were on their second when Cambell came in.

"Ten-shun, chaps," Dourian said, "it's beloved Sergeant Cambell."

Their sergeant took in the scene. "He bought it, huh?" he asked Barney.

"Yep. We can all go home."

"First thing I'm going to do," Dourian said, "is take Amanda to a shooting gallery and win her ten boxes of chocolates."

"Take the Weatherby," Loder suggested. "You'll win them all with one shot."

"That's a point," Barney said. "I guess the weapons are ours; although I don't see myself hanging a submachine gun in the den."

Cambell told him they'd be crazy to keep any of it. "Put it all into a sack and dump it in the lake. But I'd do it in the morning. You don't want to leave a Claymore for somebody to walk into."

Dourian had made a drink and offered it to Cambell. "Come on, join the office party."

"No, thanks. I want to get out of here tonight. I'll have to take the van, which means you'll have to hoof it up the road and hitch a ride." Barney left the room briefly and came back with an envelope, which he handed to Cambell.

242

"We're square," he said.

Cambell shoved it into a back pocket, hardly glancing at it. "Sorry you paid for nothing."

"Don't be. That'd be like buying a snake-bite kit and complaining that you didn't get to use it."

Cambell started to move toward the door. "Okay then."

"Wait a second." Barney searched for an easy way of saying it. "Um, thanks, huh?"

Cambell frowned. "I didn't do it for free, mister." He walked from the room and out of the cabin.

Dourian raised his glass. "Well, thank you and good night. Jesus, the guy's colder than an ice-maker."

"You should know the man by now," Barney said. "He's not the type to fraternize."

"Yeah, but still. . . ." Dourian seemed genuinely hurt. "We've been practically living in each other's pockets for a week. He could have at least stayed two minutes longer for a drink."

Loder explained something. "Cambell's a pro, and pros don't like amateurs. They understand your lack of talent but they still despise you for it. He doesn't want to hang around with us, he wants to get a long way away."

"You're right, Tom," Barney said. "We also forced him to work for money we knew he needed, and that's not guaranteed to get you liked by anybody." They discussed Cambell for a while, then heard the van start up and fade down the road. In the corner the detector console bleeped as it picked up the van and re-minded them of the equipment they had to dispose of and the work that was needed on the two cabins. They decided to take Cambell's advice and start the next morning.

An hour later the party atmosphere had evaporated and been replaced by a deep weari-ness. They were thinking about hitting the sack when the console bleeped again and a dial lit up.

They looked questioningly at each other.

"Must be Cambell coming back," Loder said.

They went outside. Far away they heard the sound of an engine coming closer. They picked up the glow of its lights through the trees, but instead of entering the loop of the road, it turned off short and they heard it backing into the forest.

"What the hell's he doing?" somebody said.

A figure came up the slope toward them. The man asked a question while he was still a good ten yards away.

"You started taking things down yet?"

"No, we're going to do it in the morning. Why?"

Cambell moved into the light. "Because they're here."

"Who's here?"

It didn't register for a moment; then all of them spoke together.

"The Pachones?"

"How do you know?"

244

"They passed me coming from Lake George. I turned around and overtook them. Four black Caddies, heavy ones."

"But the deal. . . ." Barney was thunderstruck. "The clerk told me Ripoll accepted the deal."

Loder looked from one to the other. "How did he find us?"

"I can't answer any of that. All I can tell you is they'll be here any minute."

"Christ," Dourian breathed. "What are we going to do?"

Cambell's head snapped around at him. "What I trained you to do."

Barney still wouldn't accept it. "He can't be willing to give up all that money. Maybe he just wants to talk."

Cambell spoke harshly. "Now understand this. Those men are coming here to kill you. The only way to stop them from doing that is to snap out of it and get ready for them."

Barney breathed deeply and settled down; it had been a hell of a shock. "All right. Listen, you'd better get out of here now. You don't want to run into them coming down the road."

"That's why I'm staying." The three men stared at him. "I got a flat coming in. I can't change it in time."

"Then wait till they go by. Drive out then."

"They may post a guard and you don't have any weapons to spare. I'm safer here."

"Then you can walk out. You can cut through——" Barney was interrupted by a soft bleeping from the console. Four pairs of eyes riveted on it.

"They're coming slow," Cambell said. "We've got maybe five minutes. Dourian, up on the roof. I'll handle the launcher and the A.T. Rivers, try to get a count on how many of them rush you. And watch out for those trip wires." As he reeled off the orders, he checked their weapons quickly, then picked up the grenade launcher and loaded it. He looked up to see them all standing still, watching him.

"Gentlemen," he said softly. "We have guests."

Dourian grabbed the big rifle and his ammunition and started up the ladder. Barney strapped on the forty-five, stuck the revolver and the flashlight into his belt and went out of the door running. As he moved through the gap in the spiked ditches, the lights flicked out in the cabin and he heard Cambell, running behind him, turn off and head for the hole.

He made the little cabin, stepped up through the cut door, and crossed to the window. His eyes had adjusted to the dark now, but it wasn't much help. There was no moon and the stars were mostly obscured by cloud. He waited in the silence that was broken only by the frogs in the lake and the night noises of birds. Then, far away, he heard it, the squish of tires on a rocky road, and, pinned beneath it, the low murmur of car engines. He strained for a glimpse of movement. It was a long time coming but when it did it chilled him. It would have been far less unsettling if they'd arrived in a squeal of brakes, with guns blazing, than the way they did: the heavy Cadillacs creeping forward like a funeral procession, their lights out, a terrible menace inherent in their slow approach. The first two cars stopped in front of the fence, parallel to it; the third, Ripoll's, moved in behind them, and the fourth completed the wall shielding him.

Barney reached a hand for the battery switch and stabbed it down. The flashlight in the big tree sprang on and lit up the cars. Barney picked up the walkie-talkie and pressed the talk button. "Ripoll. There's a walkie-talkie under the light."

He heard his words crackling back to him. He wondered how they sounded on the walkie-talkie back in the cabin and the one Cambell had in the foxhole, whether the fine trembling that was running through his body was showing up in his voice, too.

"Ripoll," he said again "Under the flashlight."

He took his thumb from the button and heard static; then Ripoll's voice spoke to him. It sounded just as quietly assured as it had on the phone. "Can you hear me, MacDonald?"

"I hear you, Ripoll. I also heard the clerk at the hotel. He told me you accepted the deal."

"Ah. But you know how hotel clerks are. Some are not dependable."

"It doesn't make sense, Ripoll. Nobody throws away a fortune like you're doing."

"I'm not throwing it away."

That stopped Barney; was the man here to

deal after all? Or didn't he believe him? "I don't understand. I wasn't kidding about those arrangements. You lay a finger on me and my lawyer sends a letter to the bank. The money disappears."

He heard Ripoll chuckle; no mirth in it, just contempt.

"I saved your lawyer the trouble, Señor. I simply did your trick. I obtained a specimen of your signature from the bank and wrote the letter they were expecting from you. The money is on its way back to Switzerland. And this time only the account number will release it."

It was a staggering revelation and it floored Barney. His whole position had been swept away, and so easily! And he hadn't seen it coming, that was the grinding, frustrating part— he'd thought himself so goddamn clever coming up with the idea that he'd never stopped to realize that Ripoll could work it in reverse.

"You played me and you lost, MacDonald. And when a man loses to me he loses everything."

Barney took a tighter grip on the revolver. "You may have trouble, Ripoll. I'm not up here alone."

Barney heard him give a fast order in Spanish, then the car doors opened and the Pachones poured out.

"Neither am I, Señor."

Barney played for time as he counted them quickly. "You can only kill me once, Ripoll."

There were twenty-four of them. Their blank, robot faces stared at the cabin.

"You're wrong again. You have a wife and two children; so I can kill you four times, Mr. Rivers."

The use of his name shocked Barney as much as the threat against his family. Ripoll had worked incredibly fast.

"You can forget my family, Ripoll. They're a hundred miles away where you'll never find them."

"You need a new map, Rivers. Diamond Point is only half an hour from here."

It was as if something physical had reached out from the radio and seized him in a paralyzing grip. His mind was temporarily blank, wiped clean like a slate, his body frozen. He knew! *Ripoll knew!* The words struggled from his throat. "You'll never touch them. You'll never leave here alive."

"That's very doubtful, Señor. But I don't have to move to touch them. I just left a man there. His name's Manolo. A little crazy, perhaps, but an artist with the knife."

If Barney had been holding the machine gun instead of the thirty-two he would have ruined the plan right then. Rushing on top of the cold horror that iced his heart, an instant, blood-red rage overwhelmed him and he emptied the revolver wildly into the night, firing in a crazy-blind attempt to obliterate the man in the car.

It was over in a few seconds. He came to,

dimly aware of the heavy noise of a thirty-eight, the overhead light smashing out, and the gun in his hand clicking on empty chambers. Amazingly, he'd done exactly as he was supposed to do.

He saw vague shapes moving toward him, running low, and he watched them come, hypnotized by their fast movement and the soft scuff of their shoes on the grass.

They were almost on top of him and would have found him like that if the walkie-talkie hadn't startled him out of it. It was Ripoll enjoying himself. "I still seem to be alive, Rivers. And you seem to be out of ammunition."

Barney fumbled at the flashlight, turned and dashed to the door. He hit the button and was bringing it up when it was knocked spinning from his hand as he collided with the man who'd come around the back of the cabin. Both of them went down and it was only Barney's momentum that saved him. It carried him forward, pitching him into the hole. But even as he tumbled into it, he was clawing at the holster on his hip, certain that Cambell couldn't possibly have seen his signal.

The other man had rolled onto his feet and was coming up in a crouch, a big thirty-eight in his hand coming up with him. When he saw that he had all the time in the world, he relaxed and stood up and thus ended his life. Barney heard three sounds that he couldn't separate, so closely did they follow each other: the loud boom of the launcher, then a noise like a sledgehammer hitting a melon as the man's face seemed to turn inside out, then a deafening explosion that rocked the ground as the grenade struck the inside wall and blew the cabin apart.

The concussion flattened Barney like a giant hand, and he hugged the earth as whole sections of the cabin's rear wall cartwheeled over his head. Stunned, his eyes full of dirt and his ears singing, it was sheer fright that got his legs moving underneath him, propelling him out of the hole and across the slope to the pines.

He ran down the trail, wiping at his eyes and trying to swallow the buzz out of his head. He thought he heard a single shot from Loder's gun but couldn't be sure. He left the trail, steering clear of the trip wires and bolted in through the side door of the cabin.

Dourian wasn't on the roof and Loder wasn't at the window; they were arguing with Cambell in the middle of the floor, shouting at him. "Now! We've got to go now!" Loder's voice was tinged with panic. "We can't stay here, we've got to——"

"Amanda's up there! We'll circle around——"

"*Shut up!*" It was the first and only time they heard Cambell raise his voice. "You crazy? To save your families you have to save yourselves. The only way to do that is to make this work. Now calm down and think what you're doing." It killed the shouting and Cambell went on quickly. "That man is probably waiting for Ripoll to get through here. So if we stop Ripoll

251

we stop the man." It made sense. Even through their fear they saw it. The only hope they had was that the crazy knifer would wait for Ripoll before he moved. It was only a supposition on Cambell's part, but it held out hope and they snatched at it. He didn't give them a chance to reconsider; he started barking orders. "Loder, single shots at the cabin, move! Dourian, get up there. Rivers, you get a look at them?"

"Twenty four."

Loder's gun fired once.

"How many rushed you?"

"Three maybe. And one around the back." The memory of the Pachone's face caved in by the grenade left him unaffected. He was numb to any sense of feeling toward Ripoll and his men. The hatred and the rage had died, leaving a cold practicality in its place. There were two jobs to be done, and that man dying, however horribly, merely made the first one a little easier.

Cambell crouched by Barney's window as Loder's gun fired again. This shot did the job. Something crashed through the pine of the front wall, spanged as it punctured the iron sheeting and buried itself in one of the boxes. It was powerful enough to shift the box back a few inches.

"Center left. You got him, Dourian?"

"Got him."

"Loder, try it again and keep down."

Loder fired, then sprang back behind the boxes. Two rifles replied this time, one of them firing twice in succession, the shots bracketing the window opening and raising puffs of earth from the boxes.

The Weatherby fired twice from the roof, two loud crashes hyphenated by the bolt slamming back and forth.

Down the slope the two rifles were joined by a third, and half a dozen slugs chipped hunks out of the roof and chimney.

"Dourian, slow down. Go after them one at a time."

Dourian knew his mistake, too; he'd tried to match their rate of fire. He got a grip on himself, worked a round into the chamber and brought the rifle slowly up to his shoulder. He aimed at a spot in the darkness where he knew the first rifleman was firing from, and when Loder fired again and the rifles replied, he only had to correct a fraction to the right as he squeezed the trigger. Gage had been right about the cars being bombproof; the entire passenger compartments were surrounded by a cocoon of heavy steel. But the cars' hoods and the trunks were unprotected, and the rifle that Dourian aimed at was being fired from behind the hood of the last car in line.

The huge bullet, exploded from its cartridge by the double powder charge, covered the distance from the cabin roof to the car at almost three times the speed of sound. It pierced the Cadillac just above the wheel arch, sliced through the plates of a battery, severed the carburetor from the air filter, and punched through the opposite fender. It entered the man's body on the right side of his sternum, striking a rib and breaking it off. The bronze jacket of the slug was still in place but torn and jagged, and it bit into the bone and carried it through his right lung, snapped two of the back ribs, and pushed it all ahead of it as it exited through the man's back.

Because of the darkness, and because he was the last man in line, nobody saw him flung back and belted to the ground. In the front seat the driver had felt the car rock and he got out. He saw the body lying crumpled and twisted yards away and didn't understand it; a lucky shot, but what was it doing over there? He certainly didn't connect the thunking shake of the car with the dead man. He ran over and picked up the rifle, patted the dead man's pockets for a new clip, fed it in, and ran back to the Cadillac. He leveled the rifle over the roof of the car and waited for a muzzle flash. There were two rifles out there; a big one above a small one. When the smaller one fired, he swung onto the flash and jerked three fast shots at it. The trigger was closing on the fourth when something thumped him in the stomach and sent him sprawling, the sound of bursting glass in his ears.

He couldn't seem to breathe and he lay there amazed. He'd had this feeling before, years ago in Cabrera when a horse had kicked him. He died wondering how such a thing could happen to him here.

This second casualty didn't go unnoticed; there were at least five men who saw it happen. But it escaped the attention of a sixth who was crouching with his rifle behind a tree. His attention was fixed on the rifle far away up the slope, not the one that fired so loudly, the smaller one he couldn't seem to silence. There was a frightened amateur behind that gun, he knew it by the sound of the weapon, a high-powered twenty-two, and by the way the shots splayed everywhere. When the gun fired again, he straddled the flash with four shots. From behind the security of the big pine, he saw an answering flash from the other rifle but never heard it. The bullet drilled through the tree and slammed him against the one behind it with a force that broke his shoulder. But he didn't know it; there was no pain to tell him. Four rifles had been firing, now there were only two. A man got out of Ripoll's car to find out why. When he saw the three bodies and their gaping wounds, he hurried back to report. He held a fast conversation, then called an order. The men who'd been crouching down behind the cars broke into two groups and ran in a crouch in opposite directions. They melted into the pines on either side of the slope, found the trails, and, with guns in their hands, began to advance on the cabin.

"Three down," Cambell said. He was talking about the riflemen and Barney, hunched behind the boxes, asked him how he knew.

"Different pattern."

When Dourian and Loder fired together, Barney saw what he meant: There was only one flash from the left, the other three rifles got off four shots each, which plowed into the roof. The single shot smashed into the chimney and brought an exclamation from Dourian; a very near miss.

"Hold your fire, Loder. They know who's doing the damage now."

As Cambell said it, the detector console started to bleep. Their heads jerked around at it. The needles in two of the gauges were flickering and the glass buttons next to them pulsated red. The signal was stronger on the third dial and Loder watched as the needle rose and the button brightened. By his reckoning they were almost on top of the clearing on the right, yet Cambell had made no move toward the firing switch. The needle jumped alarmingly. What in God's name was he waiting for?

"Cambell. Look at the gauge."

The reply was almost conversational. "I see it."

The Pachones coming up the right side trail were led by one of Ripoll's lieutenants. He'd earned this status by the way in which he'd taught a lesson to a man who'd bad-mouthed Ripoll: He'd taken the man's wife, soaked her hair in gasoline, and lit it. The man never bothered Ripoll again, and Ripoll had rewarded such efficiency.

The men followed him, moving swiftly through the pines that protected them from the sporadic rifle fire coming from up the slope. The trail snaked through the thick barricade of trees and ahead he saw the thickness break up as the trail opened. Immediately he stopped, halting the men behind him. He crept forward, approaching cautiously.

It was a small clearing.

He could see the trees closing in again on the other side. It bothered him. The forest was quiet but the clearing was quieter, as if there were something in it, waiting. He could smell the fresh earth, the drying sap of the newly cut trees, make out the flattened stumps on the ground. It looked innocent but it smelled of danger.

He motioned for the man behind him, muttered something to him and watched him make his way carefully across the open space. The man reached the other side; nothing happened. But still he hesitated. He sent two more men across, together this time. Nothing. He relaxed and motioned for the remaining two men to follow him and started into the clearing.

He was halfway across when the feeling washed over him again, much stronger now. And then he saw it—something small and dark protruding from a tree; something that didn't belong in the pines. His eyes riveted on it and, for the briefest instant, a blinding white flash seared his vision.

Being in front of the other two men, he took most of the blast. Almost half of the steel marbles riddled his body before the blast picked him up, picked the two men up with him, and somersaulted them back across the open space. The three who'd made it to the other side stared at the ruined bodies. They looked like paper dolls that had been shredded and crumpled up and straightened out again.

With no change of expression, no alarm, no fear, no surprise, they turned away and continued up the trail.

When the group in the pines on the other side heard the explosion, they stopped. The trees had blocked off any flash, but it had seemed to come from across the slope and maybe a little ahead of them. The leader wondered about it: wondered if there was a trail like this one on the other side and whether that explosion had been waiting for the other group. Ahead the trail danced through the trees and disappeared in the darkness. He didn't trust it; they weren't following it, it was leading them. He broke his group into two's and they went down it warily, hugging the sides, walking very lightly. They covered twenty yards like this, then came to the clearing.

As his counterpart had done, the leader halted, thrown by the sudden change in the forest. He sent a man ahead skirting the perimeter; he found the small green box sticking into the tree and called the leader over. The leader examined it, spotted the circuitry on the back and made a guess about that explosion: there was a booby trap waiting for them up ahead; this box was a sensor to pick up their approach.

They worked the box loose, pulled it out and laid it on the ground. The leader signaled the others to follow him and left three of them behind to destroy the box.

They were stomping in its plastic front with heavy, earth-shaking kicks when, back in the cabin, Cambell's fingers rotated a switch.

When the roar of the explosion died away, the rifle fire died with it and a nervous silence started up, as if each side was straining to hear what the other was doing.

Cambell left the console and squinted through the window. The remains of a fire spluttered around what was left of the little cabin, but the flames were too feeble to throw any light. Everything was still, unmoving blackness.

Cambell spoke quietly. "Rivers, Loder. Automatic. Watch the trip wires." The ringing was still in Barney's ears and his eyes smarted. He hated the darkness; it was hiding the Pachones. They had no way of knowing how effective the Claymores had been; maybe there were fifteen men creeping toward them and maybe they were very close. Cambell didn't know, why didn't he find out? Barney moved his left foot around a box and felt it bump against the flare pistol he'd laid on the floor. Why didn't Cambell let him use that? Or fire the flare in the ground? He turned from the window. "Cambell. . . ."

"Watch your sector!"

The words knifed through the cabin and Barney jerked his head back. There was still only blackness.

The two groups, their numbers cut in half, six men in all, had both done the same thing: stepped off the booby-trapped trails and kept moving forward. They sifted through the pines, traveling slowly and, at about the same time, found the trees beginning to thin out. The trails they were skirting faded away, and from the gaps in the trees they made out the dark shape of the cabin against the darker backdrop of the cliff.

Until then they hadn't known where the rifles were seated. Looking at it now, quiet, waiting, they could see that the men inside must have erected some kind of barricade, which meant they'd have to work in close with their guns, under the windows or in through one of the sides. But it would mean breaking cover.

On the left side the leader picked a tree thirty feet away, set himself, then started toward it in a fast run. He made his cover, turned and waved the next man on.

As the man stepped out between two pines his foot snagged on something and he stumbled.

Above him, with a cold, clear, merciless intensity, a light sprang on.

The lull in the action had given them time to think again about the cabin at Diamond Point and the maniac with the knife. The fear jellied their bones and pinched at their insides. Barney's hands gripped the submachine gun in an effort to choke the horrendous thought from his mind. Still, when the flashlight lit the stumbling man, he'd fired a burst before he knew it. It was as if Cambell had suddenly jerked a target up in front of him; his grip relaxed and his finger caught at the trigger in a brief hug. The first burst sent the man twirling sideways, the second was wasted on a dead man as he pitched forward on his face. Then somebody shot the light out and the darkness moved in again.

On Loder's side a man was already running. He'd seen what had happened and, even as he felt his ankle catch on the wire, he was turning and firing at the light that blasted down at him.

It was a good shot, off balance as he was, but although it smashed the flashlight it wasn't much good to him. The four bullets from Loder's gun ripped through him and he died at the same time the light did.

The bursts of machine-gun fire brought the Pachones' rifles back into play. Although the M Sixteens had flash suppressors on their muzzles, it still gave the Pachones something to shoot at and the bullets crashed into the gun ports, filigreeing the corrugated iron and knocking the boxes sideways. Each time a box was hit, it reduced its effectiveness as a bullet trap, the earth spilling from the holes punched out of the cardboard. A couple of the slugs thumped against the griddle-plate backings.

The Weatherby replied instantly but with no effect; it was evident that the rifles were being fired from behind the body of the cars where the protective armor-plating was. The jacketed bullets were possibly penetrating one side but not the other.

"Dourian," Cambell yelled. "Forget the rifles, try for the engines."

The rifles fired again and under cover of the fire a man on Barney's side made his move. He high-stepped through the trees, missed two trip wires but caught the third. When the light burst over him he dived for the ground, rolled, came up in a half-crouch, and lunged for the safety of a tree two strides away.

Three bullets from Barney's gun, small, slim, needle-nosed for high velocity, beat him by a step and the man spilled over in a tangle of arms and legs. Barney jerked back as bullets sprayed his window and Dourian, taking the flashes as coming from the middle of the cars, moved his aim down and to the left. He got off two fast shots and ducked away from the answering fire as the flagstones took a beating. He fired a third time, reloaded, and got off two more. His shooting was all based on guesswork, but one of the shots paid off. The slug plowed into a car just behind the fender, hitting the cylinder head so hard the concussion blew the hood off its catch, lifting it inches into the air. The Cadillac was mortally wounded and bled a pool of black oil, but it was still operational, as they found out a minute later.

Ripoll had no way of knowing what the two explosions had meant, but there was no question about the machine guns. And when the heavy rifle started trying to knock out the cars there was only one thing he could do. And Cambell knew it.

The cabin was too far away for him to hear the engines start up, or hear the sound of the rickety fence snapping as the heavy Cadillacs rolled through it. But he heard something that told him as much: The bleeper on the console responding to the sensor thirty yards from the fence. The needle in the bottom gauge fluttered into life and the bulb next to it began to glow. Without taking his eyes off it, Cambell reached down and got his hands on the antitank launcher, untelescoped it, and connected up the two side terminals.

The needle rose and went crazy and Cambell smacked a hand down onto the battery switch taped to the console. The current shot down the wire and detonated the flare buried in front of the left side ditch. There was a soft pop and a spurt of white light, then the next moment the lower slope was awash in a brilliant incandescence. It silvered the two cars coming toward them—one hugging the pines on the side, the other further back, over near the burned-out cabin.

It wasn't hard to imagine the sight from the viewpoint of the two drivers: a long glittering row of steel-pointed stakes opening up in front of them waiting to shred their tires. Immediately the lead car braked hard and swerved to its left, the stakes only feet from its wheels. The driver spotted the gap and went for it. Cambell, at Barney's window, had the tube resting on his shoulder, sighting along it. He tracked with the big car presenting him now with a three-quarter shot, as good as he was going to get, but his hand didn't move on the plunger. Involuntarily, Dourian cried out. "Get him now!"

But Cambell had seen something. The second car had also turned and was heading for the gap, the two cars converging on it from opposite directions. The car closest to them would be through the gap in a moment and turning.

"Cambell!" Loder yelled.

There was a loud whoosh from the tube and a burned chemical smell and, right on top of it, from out on the slope, a cataclysmic explosion that tried to tear down the sky.

The rocket struck the Cadillac low down between the doors, lifted it clear off the ground and bowled it over like a die rolled from a cup. The two men in the front seat of the second car got a brief picture of a three-ton wall of steel tumbling toward them and dived for the floor.

The armor-plating saved them. With a tremendous grinding crash, the other Cadillac smashed down onto their hood, top first, squashing the entire front of the car and bursting open the doors as if a bomb had gone off inside. As the car went from forty m.p.h. to zero, the rear end jackknifed up and thumped down again, snapping the rear axle like a stick.

Flames started up, taking over from the dying flare, and lit the two men clambering out of the second car. They crouched behind the sprung doors and opened up with rifles. From forty yards out the powerful Remingtons tore into the cabin and ripped hell out of the boxes.

"Hold your fire," Cambell yelled.

It was pointless risking a return fire; those men were sitting on an explosion. They had a choice of betting that the gas tanks wouldn't blow or trying their luck in a run for the pines. It wasn't much of a choice; a bullet can miss, an explosion can't.

They tried it with teamwork. The one on the left, with a fresh clip, laid down a barrage of covering fire while his partner broke for the trees on the right. With an automatic rifle it might have worked, but the Remington he was firing only held four shots and the barrage was over too soon. It stopped while the running man was still twenty feet short of the pines. Loder missed him once, then laid down a sustained burst ahead of him and simply let the man run into it. The bullets kicked him sideways, his legs looped up and over, and he landed on his back like a swatted insect. The other man started firing again and Barney raked the car door but couldn't pierce the armor-plating.

The man must have known he was on borrowed time; the ruined car, lying bottom up on the crushed hood, was still burning, and the tanks could go any second.

He made his decision.

He slid over the shattered glass of the front seat, pumped a shot at the cabin and started to run. Both machine guns fired, then stopped, their magazines empty. Barney and Loder fumbled in the dark, inverted the triple magazines, and tried to insert a fresh one. They tried to do it too fast. The man was going to make the trees.

"Dourian," Cambell called.

On the roof, Dourian only had time to snap off one shot. It was from a fresh clip he'd just loaded and it was a dumdum. The shot missed the running man's body but caught his left wrist. The same shot from another rifle would have broken the wrist but still left a gunman on his feet and able to kill. But when the soft point struck the bone, the lead at the tip of the slug expanded and flattened up on itself and was driven through the man's wrist like an axe, severing the hand instantly. The man gained the shelter of the pines aware only of a hot, stinging sensation. The real pain was in his right side where he'd cracked a rib in the crash.

He stood with his back to a tree recovering his breath, listening to his heavy breathing and the soft, fountaining sound that was coming from somewhere. It had been hot in the burning car, hot racing for cover; but it was cool under the trees, icy almost.

He sat down slowly as the shock stole over him, a chilled mist that moved up through his body. As the numbness seeped into his brain the cars exploded.

His final thought was that he'd made the right choice.

There were three men in the pines, two on the right, one on the left. They'd seen the cars destroyed, and the men in them, and waited. In the blaring light of the explosion when the tanks blew, they'd got a good look at the cabin; the windows had been turned into gun ports, iron sheeting around them. They'd fortified the front but probably not the sides. The man on the roof had a chimney to protect him. Their thirty-eights weren't going to be enough; they needed rifles, and they knew where there were two of them.

The man on the left stayed where he was. The two on the right ran back up the trail, found the man slumped under the tree and took his rifle and ammunition. One of them crawled to the body lying out on the slope, got that rifle and continued in a crouching run to the wrecked cars. The explosion had blown itself out, tiny blue flames burning on tires. The cars had been lifted apart, one of them stacked on its side. He hauled himself up and into the car through the gaping rear door that was now facing the sky.

He poked the rifle through the shattered opera window in the rear. Now *he* had a gun port. And he was surrounded by two-inch armor-plate.

He settled down to wait for his partner to get in position.

"Dourian, you see anything?"

"Nothing."

"Maybe that's it," Loder said.

Four bullets crashed through the side wall, cracking through the cabin inches from their backs. They hit the floor together and stayed there as another bracket punched hunks out of the side wall, powered through the center wall and smashed glass and crockery in the kitchen.

Instantly, another rifle started up, this one out on the slope, and hacked at the chimney.

It was evident what had happened: One of the Pachones had sidestepped the trip wires and had set himself up opposite their window-less, unprotected right side. The Weatherby couldn't touch him because his partner had Dourian pinned down. With a steady hail of bullets straddling the chimney, there was no way Dourian could get a shot off. The man out there could take his time, riddle the side wall, and sooner or later he'd get them. Cambell moved fast. He grabbed at some boxes, tumbled three of them away from the wall and sprang into the niche he'd made for himself. When they lived through the next barrage, Barney and Loder did the same, brought their guns up and half emptied them at the side wall. When the rifle replied, they knew exactly where he was: behind the big pine ten yards from the cabin, a pine too thick for the machine guns.

"Dourian, can you see him?"

"No."

A quartet of bullets chunked into the chimney. Two of them caught a join, penetrated the old mortar, and spanged against the lead pipes inside. Cambell and Dourian yelled back at each other.

"Where's the other guy?"

"Behind a wrecked car."

The rifles fired at the voices and they huddled against their cover. The iron sheeting was cold on Barney's back. That and the thin pine of the front wall was all that stood between them now and the rifleman out on the slope. If he decided to switch his fire from Dourian, he'd drill them before they even knew it. Even as it was, the man at the side might get to them anyway; the boxes of earth, which had already taken a pounding, no longer had the iron sheeting to take the sting out of the slugs and were coming apart. When the bullets struck them, they ripped the weakened cardboard and sent clouds of stinging dirt spraying through the cabin. The earth, leaking from the boxes, lost its tight, compact strength, and the griddle plates, side on to the fire now, were useless.

There followed a concentrated five seconds when the room became a madhouse of dirt and fumes and noise, sharp splinters of flying wood and whining bullets biting through the air. The trap they'd so carefully prepared had been turned against them. They were fish in a barrel.

Above the hammering of the guns, Dourian heard Cambell calling to him. "Give me the rifle. Jacketed rounds."

Dourian didn't stop to wonder what he could possibly do with it down there. He slapped in a fresh clip and shoved the rifle, butt forward, halfway over the hole.

Instead of staggering his shots, the rifleman at the side was firing in four-round bursts, which was a mistake. It gave Cambell a chance to move on the reload. As the fourth shot from a new barrage sounded, Cambell yelled, *"Okay!"* and Dourian let the rifle go.

Cambell lunged out from the wall, caught it, and tumbled onto the floor. There was no stopping and starting in his action; as he rolled onto his stomach he already had the rifle into his shoulder and was firing. It was a phenomenal piece of shooting; he handled the ten-pound rifle like a kid's twenty-two, overriding the heavy recoil, smothering it with his body, working the bolt back and forth so fast his three shots sounded like one long one. He knew exactly where the big pine was and could see, even in the dim light of the room, gaping bullet holes that gave him a line, but he was still firing blind.

It worked, though. With a soldier's uncanny instinct for the enemy, the three shots tore out an entire section of the side wall, punctured the big pine, and killed the man who was firing be-hind it.

With the rifle on their flank silenced, it was all over for the man in the car. Barney and Loder leaped to the windows and got a perfect target when he fired at the chimney.

They unloaded the rest of their second magazines, thirty-four rounds in all. It was like a metal storm hitting the car. If the man had chosen to remain behind it, instead of climbing inside, he would have weathered it. But being surrounded by armor-plating put him inside a steel cage. When five of the slugs zipped through the rear window, they ricocheted crazily around the interior, banking off the metal roof and sides like balls in a pinball machine, three of them angling through his body twice before plowing into the upholstery.

There was no more firing. Barney assumed that all the Paohones were out of action.

"Let's go!" he cried and started for the door, Loder close behind him, Dourian with a foot on the ladder.

Cambell halted them with one sharp word. He was back on his feet by the window.

Watching him stare into the night, Barney knew that he was sensing more than he was seeing, soaking information through his skin, waiting for something to register on his nerve ends.

Cambell said softly, "Dourian, throw me a clip."

Dourian dropped it down to him. Cambell slipped the clip into the rifle and froze.

"Something," he murmured.

They listened, straining. The night pressed against the cabin with an iron stillness, not even a wind to move the trees. After the deafening bangs of the Weatherby, shattering in the enclosed space, they heard only vibration in their ears. With soft clicks, Barney and Loder inverted their magazines.

"Rivers." Cambell's voice, very low. "Get the flare pistol."

Barney found it buried under a pile of boxes and got a hand on it. He still didn't know what was bugging Cambell, but he wasn't about to ask questions now. There wouldn't have been time for that anyway, because there was another man with a gun in his hand in the cabin, and he was already making his move.

It was the third man who'd waited on the left. He'd crept up on the cabin and sneaked in through the bedroom door just as the one on the other side had opened up with the rifle. He'd almost walked into the bullets and had waited out the rifle fire lying flat on his face in the kitchen, glasses and plates shattering around him. He'd been in there, a few feet away from them, all that time.

They almost found out about him the hard way.

Three men standing close together is not a hard target, and Dourian, on the roof, was with-

272

out a weapon. The Pachone would have got all four of them.

But Barney was turned toward his left and caught the tiny squeak of movement from the door. It was the briefest of warnings and it didn't really register on his brain. When the door jerked open, his body did his thinking for him and the flare pistol whipped up and exploded.

There's nothing much slower than a flare from a ten-gauge pistol, but with only a few feet separating them the speed didn't matter. The heavy cartridge struck the man in the chest, sending him reeling back through the door, his own gun firing into the ceiling as he went over. The flare bounced off his body, slammed into the wall, fell to the floor, and rolled. It came to rest against the man who was trying to get to his feet. He was still trying when the flare detonated.

Three hundred feet up it would have been just a pretty pop in the sky, but twenty feet away in the next room the flare was a stunning blast that blew out searing white rockets of exploding phosphorus.

The kitchen became an instant caldron of flames that shot through the door and climbed the walls of the room, the old, dried-out pine going up like paper.

They grabbed at boxes, tumbled them down. The iron sheeting, weakened by the rifle fire, pulled away in a moment and they leaped through the front door.

Dourian jumped from the roof and together they bolted down the slope. They ran through the gap in the ditch, past the wreck of the cars, Dourian snatching up the rifle the man inside had dropped.

The flames from the cabin lit up the slope, back-lit them, but they ran upright straight down the middle, certain that there was only one more man to beat—Ripoll's bodyguard. They knew what he'd do when he saw them, get his boss out of there in a hurry, and they needed Ripoll to halt the crazy man at the cabin.

With fifty yards to go, they heard a heart-stopping sound: the whir of a car's starter. It had to be Ripoll's car. Parked as it had been behind the other three, it had been protected from the gunfire, but apparently, from the way the engine was refusing to catch, the protection hadn't been a hundred percent. They ran faster and harder, but they were still thirty yards away when the engine caught and roared.

There was a squeal of tires getting a grip; then the car slewed away and vanished around the loop of the road behind the pines. They were going to have only one chance at it; it would be in the open for no more than fifty feet when it came out again. After that it'd be gone. Cambell skidded to a halt and dropped to one knee, the others dashing by him, their one overriding thought to reach that car. Yet when Cambell shouted at them to get down, the solid week of training had programmed them to obey his voice and they dived to the ground and rolled.

Faintly lit by the blazing cabin, the big Cadillac charged out from behind the pines, the rear wheels still screaming for purchase on the rocky road. Cambell, hunched over the Weatherby, picked the car up immediately and tracked with it, opting for one good shot.

It paid off.

The rifle banged and the soft-point slug smashed into the rim of the front wheel slamming it sideways and buckling it against the arch. The heavy car collapsed on one side, skewering off the road into the trees.

They were on their feet and running, sprinting through the broken fence, bearing down on the crashed car.

The offside front door burst open and a man blundered around the back, a sawed-off pump gun swinging up.

He wasn't prepared for what he ran into.

The four men fired almost together. The two machine guns stopped the man and danced him sideways. Dourian's Remington flung him back, and a bullet from the Weatherby punched him off his feet, lifting him up and thumping him down onto the trunk of the Cadillac. He lay, stretched out on it, like a dead animal lashed to a hunter's car.

It was Barney who made the door first. He jumped through it and thrust his gun at the man who sat upright, arms folded, in the deep luxury of the back seat.

"Get out."

Ripoll, with no expression on his face, complied. He unlocked his door, which was jerked open by Loder.

Cambell and Dourian were already running back for the van. It was their best bet now, even though, Dourian remembered, they'd have to change the flat. The other Cadillac was clearly going nowhere, and Ripoll's needed more than a new wheel.

Barney brought his gun to within an inch of Ripoll's chest. "If we're too late. . . ." He could scarcely get the words out.

By contrast, Ripoll's voice was calm and measured. "I promise nothing," he said.

The machine gun stabbed into his chest. "I sure as hell do."

Then the van started up and they saw it come bucking out of the trees. There was no list to it, no floppy wheel, it tore down at them and crunched to a stop on four perfect tires.

Cambell yelled at them, they bundled Ripoll inside, jumped in themselves and the van leaped away.

"The flat," Barney said. "How did you fix the flat?"

Cambell slapped the van into third and sent it barreling up the road, bouncing and swaying around the bends. "Chewing gum," he said to the windshield.

They stared at him. There had been no flat; he'd lied to them. The realization of what he'd done astonished them, but they had no time to dwell on it now. They only had one thought in their minds.

When they reached the highway, Cambell floored the gas pedal and hurtled through the curves in a straight line. But even at their top speed they knew they couldn't make Diamond Point in less than twenty minutes. Which meant that if the man with the knife hadn't already gone into that cabin, he had another nineteen minutes to do so.

The cabin was down a short, steep side road that turned off just before the outskirts of the little town. It was just a dirt road running into grass as the property swept down to the water's edge. It was an ideal spot, private; its nearest neighbor some distance away hidden by pines. The cabin itself was double-storied with a big old-fashioned porch running around it. It faced the lake, lovely now in the late hours, a mere suggestion of breeze rippling the lights coming across the water from the towns on the opposite bank. A rowboat nudged against a small dock, tugging on its line, fishing tackle stowed under the seats. Behind the cabin a circular clothesline stood like a scarecrow, towels and swimsuits hanging from it. There was an old stone barbecue at the side with a wooden picnic table and benches. Under the table was a plastic baseball bat and nearby a doll buggy lying on its side. Upon the porch a cane table and chairs were

set out near the screen door and at one end, between two of the posts, a canvas hammock was
strung low.

Apart from a lamp in an upstairs bedroom,
the only other point of light on the property was
a tiny red glow that brightened briefly in the
pines. The man took the cigar from his mouth
and spent a long time blowing out smoke. He
sat with his back to a tree on a raised knoll that
overlooked the cabin. He'd been watching it for
some time, watched the women putting the kids
to bed, clearing the barbecue supper, then washing up, their heads bobbing at the kitchen window. He'd heard their soft voices talking on the
porch, then the sounds of their good nights as
the downstairs lights flicked out and the ones
upstairs came on. Two of the lights had gone
out. There was just one more to go.

He held the bayonet in front of him, twisting
it in his hands, running a thumb lovingly along
the deep groove that ran down the center of
the ten-inch blade. He sucked on the cigar
again, held the blade up to the glow and studied
it, trying to decide which edge was the most
perfect. No, both sides were faultless; not a
single nick or scratch on its needle tip or its icy
edges. He never tired of admiring it. It was a
beautiful knife. Clever, too. It knew what to do
better than he did. His was just a light hand on
the grip; the blade directed itself. More of a
sword than a knife. A singing sword. It sang
when it was happy and it was happy when it
worked.

It would be singing soon. It moved in his hand, excited, anxious. It would sing to the women first, the two older ones. Something bright and gay. For the children, a lullaby, of course. The young woman it would leave till last, save its best song for her. It would play her young body like a fine guitar. A flamenco, soft at first, caressing, then building slowly to a fiery, strumming climax.

Out on the lake on the little island opposite, a camper looking at the western shore saw a light wink out. He was too far away to see another point of light, much, much smaller, extinguish a moment later.

When Amanda put the book down and switched off the light, she knew it was only a gesture. If she was lucky she'd drift off in the small hours, the same as she had all the other nights she'd been there. Sleep wasn't something that came easy when your mind was alive with the same nagging worry. She threw off the sheet and lay there in her shorty pajamas. She heard a small cry from down the hall and went to check: one of the children bothered by a bad dream. She looked in at the others, put a teddy bear into its owner's arms, and went down the hall. Soft snores came from Elaine and Peggy's rooms—a tiring job running after kids all day. She walked down the stairs and let herself quietly out of the screen door onto the porch, snapped on the yellow bug light, and tried one of the chairs. When it didn't suit her, she got up and settled on the hammock. Swinging her legs up, she stretched out and let her body relax. Behind her everything was still: the night, the lake, the pines, the hand on the porch rail.

They tore through the little town of Warrensburgh ignoring the stop signs, not even thinking about cops. The van was shuddering with speed, a shimmy starting in the wheels, the engine howling. But a minute later, Cambell stamped on the brakes and let the tires burn as he fought the van to a stop. The turnoff to Diamond Point was a minor road with a sign to match and they'd gone right by. He chunked the gears into reverse, took the van whining backward, swung it, and charged into the road heading east.

He shot a question at Barney. "How far?"

"Four miles."

Dourian thumped the seat. "Come *on!*" They were already doing eighty, but it wasn't fast enough for him. He wanted to get there now. And he had good reason to.

The porch floor was strongly built and weathered; so there was no squeak or movement when he put a foot on it and pulled himself up slowly behind the rail. In front of him the pale gold hair spilled out on the hammock; he was close enough to catch the warm woman smell of her. Her pajamas lay against her body, the white swell of her breasts showing, the nipples, tweaked by the night air, pressing against the thin fabric.

280

His eyes traveled slowly down her body, lingering on the soft scoop of her navel, the rise of her tummy, the creamy-skin thighs, beautiful creamy-skin thighs. Creamy-skin breasts and thighs.

In slow motion he curled a leg over the balustrade and began to inch his body over it. He stopped instantly when her hand jerked up and slapped at her shoulder.

The mosquito saved her life. He could have moved then—he was only a hand's reach away—but he wanted her quiet and supine, beautiful the way she'd been before. He waited for her to settle back again, but she sat up and got off the hammock. If she'd been turned a little more to the left the sight would have shocked her dumb—a few feet away, frozen motionless, a thin, dark-haired man with a smiling face yellowed by the light, and a bayonet in his hand. But she left the porch looking straight ahead and went through the screen door, leaving the bug light burning. The man stayed where he was momentarily, then dropped to the ground and padded to the front steps. It was then that the van came silently around the corner of the entrance road.

Cambell hadn't cut the engine, it was red-hot from the rough treatment and, as he'd braked hard to make the turn into the drive, it had quit on him. He let it roll, intending to start it on the gears, but when they swung onto the grass and spotted the man moving up the steps, there was no time for anything else but what Cambell did. The guns were useless; they'd never have cleared them to get a shot off. He did the only thing he could think of to stop the man—flashed the brights on and off. They saw the man whip around, surprised, uncertain.

There was still no time for a rifle. Cambell flicked the lights once, then killed them completely as he stopped the van.

It was a clever thing to do; it was the kind of imperial gesture a man like Ripoll would make, a visual snapping of the fingers to summon a subordinate. But there was no way of knowing if it would work, nothing for Barney or Loder or Dourian to do except sit there transfixed in frozen hope.

But Cambell was moving. He switched on the parking lights, then reached behind him and took the machine gun from Loder's hands. Carefully he broke the roof light with the butt, then unhooked the shoulder sling and slipped it around his neck.

They heard the soft tread of the man's feet coming toward them and Cambell slid out of the door leaving Loder's gun on the seat. It would have been an easy matter for Loder to have stepped out of the van and mowed the man down, but now the killing of him by any possible method was subordinated by the killing of him by a quiet one. The alternative was a loud burst of gunfire followed by lights in the cabin and their families spilling out onto the grass, staring with horror at the riddled body and the husband/father with a machine gun.

Thirty feet away the man stopped, expecting Ripoll's Cadillac. In the faint illumination of the parking lights, they saw him hesitate. He looked ready to turn and bolt for the cabin.

"Call him." Barney had a gun barrel at Ripoll's head. "Call his name." Ripoll obeyed. He leaned toward the window.

"Manolo. . . ."

The man came trotting up like a faithful dog. He saw the strangers and their guns, took a step backward and whirled as Cambell came around the rear of the van. The bayonet flashed up. Cambell seemed to stop and curl back, then come forward as the blade scythed through the air.

Barney thought it missed him and was sure of it when Cambell slammed his right forearm against the man's knife hand, pinning it to the side of the van. He punched with his left fist, a short, pistonlike body blow that drew a gasp from the man, pulled him around, and rode him to the ground.

For a moment they were just two tangled bodies. Then they half separated and Barney saw: Cambell had a knee in the man's back and the shoulder sling around his throat, his fists, no more than an inch apart, straining away from each other. The man flopped arms and legs for a moment, then lay still, but Cambell kept the pressure on. When he finally relaxed, he stood up and dragged the body to the rear door. He came back to the driver's seat, reached a hand into the glove compartment and took out a flashlight. He turned the wing mirror on the fender, opened his shirt, and played the light on his side.

Barney was surprised; he'd come to think of Cambell as invulnerable.

"How bad?" He couldn't see.

"I'll live."

Cambell switched off the flashlight, moved to the rear again, opened the doors. He took off his shirt, bundled it up and threw it into the back and picked up one of the newspapers Barney had bought one evening. A born teacher, he didn't seem to be able to quit.

"Newsprint," he said. "Makes a good dressing. Low bug count." He made a wad of it, pressed it against his side and bound it in place with some electrical tape. "I need a shirt. Wait, that guy's jacket will do."

Ripoll, whose stony expression hadn't changed since they'd left Little Bear Lake, looked outraged. He put a hand to the lapel of the beautifully tailored jacket; the suit must have cost him five hundred dollars.

"No," he said.

Dourian knocked his hand away and wrenched the jacket off him. "You heard the man, he wants your coat."

Cambell slipped the jacket on and buttoned it. It just about covered the paper dressing. He had Loder help him get the body into the rear, got in after it and told Dourian to get them out of there quietly. Dourian started the van on the gears, swung it up the slope and crept out of the drive. They headed south, a lot slower than they'd come, wondering what Cambell was going to do with the dead man in the back.

They found out a few miles past Lake George.

Going up a gradient, a drop of several feet each side of the road, he opened the rear doors and rolled the body out as they swung around a curve. It bounced on the road and tumbled down the incline into the side ditch. He closed the doors and searched in the back, coming up with a large canvas sack.

"There a bridge around here?" he asked.

"Glen Falls. It goes over the Hudson."

Cambell told them to give him their guns. "The holster, too, Rivers. But keep the automatic for your friend."

They passed them back. "The river isn't very deep," Barney said. "They'll find them sooner or later."

"Let 'em. They won't find any prints."

They heard the machine guns and the rifles clacking together and the sound of a drawstring closing. Fifteen minutes later, they slowed for the bridge approach.

There was very little traffic; they let a car go by, then had the bridge to themselves. Dourian stopped the van in the middle, Barney hopped out, took the sack from Cambell and dropped it over the rail into the water. Then they got out of there in a hurry and headed toward the Thruway. Now that they had nothing but the long drive ahead of them, Barney had time to think about the man sitting next to him. He was immaculate in his silk embroidered shirt, heavy silk tie, his wavy, gray-flecked hair perfectly in place. He stared severely ahead, not used to the role of prisoner and not recognizing it. The man was a lot of things, all hideous, but he was no coward.

"How did you find us, Ripoll?"

He answered but without deigning to turn his head. "You left a wide trail to Lake George. Then all I had to do was cover the real-estate people."

"The old man," Barney said. "But he didn't know about the cabin at Diamond Point."

"Neither did your neighbors. But your secretary did."

Barney nodded. His secretary; so simple. As Cambell had said, anybody could be found.

Cambell glanced at the man. "What are you going to do with him?"

"Drop him off at somebody's place. I think you know him, Ripoll. Name's Gage." He gave no sign that he'd heard. "An American who used to live in Cabrera? You killed his wife and kids." Ripoll didn't bat an eye, but Barney was saving his best shot till last. "I think I know what he'll do with you. I think he'll take you to get a little sun in Cabrera."

That brought Ripoll's head around and he looked at Barney.

Barney smiled at him. "I hear they love you down there."

There was no more talk after that. Like Dourian and Loder, Barney watched the road unwind and kept his mind a blank, unwilling yet to think about what they'd just gone through with the Pachones and how very close their families had come to a bloodbath. That would have to wait till they were in a position to take the shuddering exhaustion it would bring. They couldn't collapse yet. It was the last lap, but it wouldn't be finished till Ripoll was off their hands and out of their lives.

Just a few more hours now.

Chapter Twenty

It was getting on to three A.M. when they reached Manhattan. Even the Barrio was closing down; there was very little life showing as they pulled up outside the tenement where Gage lived.

Barney got out and motioned Ripoll to follow.

"You need some help?" Dourian asked.

Barney held up the forty-five. "I got all I need."

Ripoll squeezed out of the door and stood on the sidewalk, big and impressive.

"After you," Barney said.

Ripoll addressed Cambell. "My jacket, please."

Barney had to admit it, the man was really something. He knew he was on his way to Cabrera, and he had to know he'd be dead very soon after he got there, but he wanted to go properly dressed.

Cambell disappointed him. "You got a check for it?"

"What?"

Barney nudged the gun into him, moving him toward the stoop and the hallway with the single forty-watt bulb. Gage had said that he lived on the second floor right. They started up the stairs. Halfway up the first flight, Ripoll made his move.

"Half the money, Rivers. We stop here and half of it's yours."

"Oh, sure."

"I promise you. And whatever I promise a man he gets."

Barney put the forty-five close to the man's head and let him hear the hammer clicking back. "All I can promise you is a bullet if you don't move."

Ripoll didn't repeat his offer, but the look he gave Barney was a look of contempt for a fool.

They climbed to the second floor and Barney rapped on a door sharply. "Gage." He knocked and called again. Somebody moved inside and a fogged voice asked who it was. "It's Rivers. I've got a friend of yours out here."

There was the sound of a police lock sliding in its slot, then Gage opened the door. There was no light in the hall, but the light coming from his room was enough for him to recognize Ripoll. The rumpled look was wiped from his face and his half-closed eyes opened wide.

"I thought you'd be surprised," Barney said. He prodded Ripoll into the room, pushing past the astounded man standing there in his shorts. Gage didn't even close the door.

"How in the world. . . ?"

"I had some expert help."

Gage stared at Ripoll, who stared coldly back at him. "Where are the Pachones?"

"Out of action," Barney said.

"*All* of them?"

"That's right." Gage was having a hard time with it, but he had to accept the proof standing in front of him. "You going to take him back to Cabrera?"

Gage smiled slowly. "Nonstop."

"Then you'll need this." Barney handed him the automatic. "Because I don't think he wants to go."

Then Ripoll spoke, his voice angry, harsh. "You're three times a fool, Rivers. You got into this like a fool, by mistake. On the stairs just now you turned down a fortune, and only a fool does that. And now you've just handed this man a gun."

Barney didn't understand. A half-formed question moved on his lips, then he looked at Gage and the bottom fell out of everything. The forty-five in the man's hand wasn't pointing at Ripoll.

"I told you not to trust anybody, Rivers. Remember?" Gage had a dull, flat look on his face and no color to his voice. "I tried to warn you away, but I didn't know then what your game was and that you were already a player." It wasn't the reversed position or the threat of the gun that dumbfounded Barney as much as the sheer unexpectedness of the switch. He was totally unprepared for it. Gage had fooled him completely, a hundred and ten percent.

Ripoll was talking, fast and efficient.

"There's a van at the curb; we'll take it. There are three men in it. They have no guns, but be careful with the man wearing the jacket. The other two are amateurs." He flicked his eyes at Barney. "Kill him."

Barney heard the words but couldn't believe them; Ripoll had ordered his execution as if he were ordering a cup of coffee.

Gage moved to his right, picked up a sofa cushion and pressed it over the muzzle of the gun. He held the gun low, stomach level, and stepped up to Barney.

Barney watched it all happen as if he were a spectator outside of the action. He actually saw his death coming when Gage's finger squeezed the trigger and the hammer released. Instinct jackknifed him forward, doubled his arms in front of him, and squinched his eyes tight. He heard a loud bang but felt nothing.

It wasn't the forty-five that had gone off.

It was the Remington rifle that Cambell had fired from the door.

Gage and Ripoll were both slammed back into the room and crashed to the floor. Barney still hadn't moved, and Cambell had to do it for him. He leaped into the room, snatched up the automatic, grabbed Barney's arm and shoved him through the door. Together they clattered down the stairs, made the sidewalk and the waiting van, which took off as they jumped inside. Nobody spoke till they were blocks away and heading downtown, and it was Cambell, not Barney. Barney had received a huge shock, then had been killed and resurrected all in the space of a few minutes; it took a little getting used to.

Typically, what Cambell had to say wasn't complimentary. He checked the forty-five in his hand and shook his head as if it were a cheap plastic replica. "It's a lucky thing you're dumb, Rivers, otherwise you'd be dead." He held the gun up for Barney to see. "You forgot to cock it again."

Barney raised a hand from the seat and semaphored a shrug; just as long as he was alive. Slowly his mind unstuck and a couple of things occurred to him. He croaked out a question and got an answer from Dourian.

"Tom did. If you'd relied on me, we'd still be waiting at the curb."

Loder colored it in. "Ripoll said we'd left a wide trail to Lake George, and that bothered me. What wide trail? We were damned careful. The only person who knew was Gage; I heard you tell him on the phone. It didn't come to me till you'd gone up there."

Barney turned to Cambell. "How about the rifle? I thought they all went into the river."

"I didn't trust Ripoll. He looked like a man who was sitting on a secret."

"What about him?" Loder asked. "What happened up there?"

"I went for the man with the gun. Ripoll was standing behind him. His bad luck."

They were quiet, thinking about it. They drove south, moving through the expanse of Columbus Circle. The proximity of the hundred-thousand-dollar apartments on Central Park South reminded Dourian of the money, and he asked about it.

"Gone," Barney said.

"Gone?"

Loder knew it, too. "Gone for good. Ripoll told us himself. When he transferred it back to Switzerland, he made sure that only an account number would spring it. And you can bet Ripoll was the only one who knew that number."

"It'll just rot away in a bank?" It was a terrible thought.

"Yep. It'll join all the other unclaimed millions in Switzerland."

Barney looked at Cambell. "I guess you've pieced all this together by now. You heard Ripoll on the walkie-talkie. It can't be hard to figure."

"I got a fair idea," Cambell said.

A few minutes later, he told Dourian to stop the van. They swung off Broadway onto Forty-fifth. Except for a garage truck gulping trash down the block, it was a dead street the men got out onto.

Cambell shifted over behind the wheel and spoke to them through the window. "If you're smart, you'll check into a cheap hotel where they don't ask questions and grab a change of clothes in the morning. They're not going to let you on a train to Westchester looking like that."

They looked at one another and saw what he meant; their faces were grimy and there was dirt in their hair, their clothes oil-stained and smelling of guns. Cambell, with a face as grubby as theirs, and with the incongruous suit jacket over his bare chest, was a pretty wild sight himself. Barney asked him what he was going to do now.

"Back to the pad, lose the rifle, clear the van out and return it in the morning."

"What about your wound?"

"I know a doctor who owes me some stitches."

"That was a cute trick with the flat," Dourian said.

"Real cute." Barney picked it up; it was a nice way into a tough subject. "I don't know why you wanted to stick around, but I'm—" Cambell cut him off. His voice was as flat and as hard as they'd ever heard it.

"Now get this. You hired me to do a job. If I wanted to put in a little overtime, that's my business. Believe me, I didn't do it because I like the color of your eyes; so don't start trying to pass out any medals." He shoved the van into gear. "See you around." And he left them with that, taking the van away fast.

They watched it travel up the street, not surprised by what he'd said but stung by it all the same. When the van reached the corner, a surprising thing happened: The horn sounded, three honks, and a hand appeared out of the window, half a wave, half a salute. Then the van was gone.

Dourian shook his head in wonder, a smile starting on his face. "Son of a bitch," he said.

They turned slowly and started to trudge up the street toward a hotel, the weariness beginning to seep into their bodies.

It had been a tough week.

Epilogue

As he'd been wrong about most things during the whole episode, Barney was also wrong when he thought they'd heard the last of the matter. Fortunately, it wasn't from the authorities. When the incredible scene at Little Bear Lake had been discovered the following week, the police had had nothing to go on. With the two cabins burned to the ground, there was nothing to connect anybody with anything, and any equipment. that was left, like the sensors in the ground, had been washed clear of fingerprints by a day's rain.

The realtor couldn't help them much, nor the clerk in the store, just a general description of the four men that could have fitted a lot of people.

The Pachones were identified and their boss having already been found dead in the Barrio, it wasn't hard to put the whole thing down as a revenge action by an extremist group. In fact, an expatriate group of Cabrerans did indeed claim credit for it.

And there were no repercussions from the bank in Bronxville. Barney had been worried about that till he'd realized that it was probably Gage who'd tracked him down there, and Gage wouldn't have told the bank that anything was wrong.

As for the original twenty thousand dollars, Cambell's fee and the cost of the weapons had eaten up quite a bit of it and the rest they'd sent anonymously to the old realtor whose property they'd destroyed. So they thought the whole affair was over and done with. And it was except for the clincher.

Barney found out about that two weeks later, sitting under the beech with Tom Loder, the kids playing at the end of the garden, both families back home now.

Dourian wasn't with them. He'd closed up his house, given the key to a rental agent, and moved into an apartment in town with Amanda. Living in Manhattan and working in Hartsdale he became a reverse commuter, which he claimed was the only way to travel. They hadn't seen too much of them.

Barney, leafing through the Sunday paper, caught sight of an item that grabbed his attention and finally sagged him back in his chair.

"What happened, the Mets win?" Loder asked.

Stupefied, Barney stared at the paper. He

looked up blankly. "Of course. Oh, my God, of course."

Loder reached for the newspaper.

"Cabrera," Barney croaked. "Near the bottom."

Loder found the item, something about U.S. aid to Cabrera, skimmed through the first part, then started to read out loud. "The committee expressed concern that the island's militia is being trained by a former U.S. Army sergeant who was dishonorably discharged some years ago. The ex-sergeant . . ." Loder's voice slowed ". . . Raymond H. Cambell, was reported to be earning a salary well in excess of fifty thousand dollars a year in his new post. A spokesman for Cabrera defended this, saying that the money was coming from the country's internal budget and not from the aid program. The island apparently has been the recipient of a very large cash influx recently, the source of which remains to be identified."

Loder finished the article with the same glazed expression that Barney had. He said, carefully, "What is Cambell doing in Cabrera? And how come fifty grand a year?"

"I am so dumb," Barney said. "Dumb, dumb, dumb." He leaned forward.

"When that knifer slashed Cambell, did you see any blood?"

"No, it was too dark."

"I didn't either."

"What are you saying?"

"He wasn't wounded at all. He was faking it.

He took off what we all assumed was a blood-stained shirt. He needed something to wear over that dressing he made. He got what he was after—Ripoll's jacket." Barney closed his eyes and pressed his forehead. "Oh, boy. All the time we thought Cambell was just a hard-case soldier, but, man, he had his ears and eyes open. He knew about Ripoll transferring that money back, he heard Ripoll say so, on the walkie-talkie he had in the hole."

"But the jacket. What's with the jacket?"

"If you had a Swiss bank account and you rode around in an armored Cadillac with a couple of dozen bodyguards, where would be the safest place to keep the account number?"

In a tiny voice Loder supplied the answer. "In your wallet."

"Right. In a nice deep inside pocket of your beautifully tailored jacket."

Loder had to grapple with it; it was an awe-inspiring revelation. "But fifty thousand a year. . . . Why settle for that when he could have had millions?"

"You know Cambell as well as I do. Can you see him getting out of a Rolls in Monte Carlo? That kind of money would be as useless to him as it would have been to us. So he traded it to Cabrera in return for what he likes doing best. Playing soldiers."

Loder was nodding his head. It made sense. "He probably wrote himself a twenty-year contract."

Barney grunted and said wistfully, "It's a little unfair, Tom. Cambell ends up with a cushy job, George ends up with a cushy girl, and what do you and I end up with?"

The answer was supplied by his wife.

She came out of the house and down to the table where they were sitting. She greeted Loder, then said to Barney, "I'm sorry, honey, but the washing machine just quit again. I think it's gone for good this time."

"The washing machine," Barney said.

"I don't know how we're going to buy a new one, we're already in the red this month. I've got that budget down to the bone, but we're still spending too much money."

Barney picked up the newspaper, looked at the item at the bottom, then tossed it onto the table. He gave his wife a funny little grin.

"Yeah," he said, "I guess we're going to have to cut down."

THE BEST OF BESTSELLERS
FROM WARNER BOOKS!

A STRANGER IN THE MIRROR by Sidney Sheldon (89-204, $1.95)
This is the story of Toby Temple, superstar and super bastard, adored by his vast TV and movie public, but isolated from real human contact by his own suspicion and distrust. It is also the story of Jill Castle, who came to Hollywood to be a star and discovered she had to buy her way with her body. When these two married, their love was so strong it was—**terrifying!**

THE SUMMER DAY IS DONE by R.T. Stevens   (89-270, $1.95)
In the tradition of **Love's Tender Fury** and **Liliane** comes **The Summer Day Is Done**, the haunting story of a forbidden love between the secret agent of the King of England and the daughter of the Imperial Czar.

THE STAR SPANGLED CONTRACT   (89-259, $1.95)
by Jim Garrison
From the first crack of the rifle, former undercover agent Colin McFerrin is flung headlong into a maze of deception and death as he tries desperately to save the President from assassins within his own government. "A chilling book . . . a knowledgeable, suspenseful thriller . . . first-rate, charged with menace. It will keep you glued to the printed page."—**John Barkham Reviews**

LORETTA LYNN: COAL MINER'S DAUGHTER (89-252, $1.95)
by Loretta Lynn with George Vecsey
It's a Horatio Alger story with a country beat, "so open, honest and warm that it's irresistible."—**New York News.** 100,000 copies sold in hardcover!

W A Warner Communications Company

Please send me the books I have checked.

Enclose check or money order only, no cash please. Plus 35¢ per copy to cover postage and handling. N.Y. State residents add applicable sales tax.

Please allow 2 weeks for delivery.

WARNER BOOKS
P.O. Box 690
New York, N.Y. 10019

Name ....

Address ....

City .... State .... Zip ....

———— Please send me your free mail order catalog

THE BEST OF BESTSELLERS
FROM WARNER BOOKS!

AUDREY ROSE by Frank DeFelitta   **(82-472, $2.25)**
The novel on reincarnation. Now a Major Motion Picture! "Is it ever compulsive reading! The author . . . can unobtrusively gather up a fistful of your nerve ends, and squeeze. If **The Exorcist** was your cup of hemlock you'll be mad about **Audrey Rose.**"—**Cosmopolitan**

THE DAY BEFORE SUNRISE by Thomas Wiseman **(89-213, $1.95)**
It is April 1945. Like rats, Hitler's henchmen are scurrying to desert sinking Germany. Allen Dulles, OSS chief in Switzerland, is working secretly with the Reich's General Wolff on a scheme code-named Sunrise. Its objective is to speed the end of the war before the Russians capture more of Europe. This first-class thriller is fiction, but it's all the more terrifying because it recalls so much that was real!

LIBERTY TAVERN by Thomas Fleming   **(82-367, $2.25)**
Liberty Tavern is a rich, full-blooded saga of the Revolution that centers upon Jonathan Gifford, the proprietor of Liberty Tavern and his family. It's a story abundant in romance and heroism. **The Gone With The Wind of the War of Independence!**

SYBIL by Flora Rheta Schreiber   **(82-492, $2.25)**
over 5 million copies in print! A television movie starring Joanne Woodward, Sally Field and Martine Bartlett! A true story more gripping than any novel of a woman possessed by sixteen separate personalities. Her eventual integration into one whole person makes this a "fascinating book."—**Chicago Tribune**

W A Warner Communications Company

THE BEST OF BESTSELLERS
FROM WARNER BOOKS!